Champions Don't Cry

by Nan Gilbert

Cover by Ruth Sanderson

SCHOLASTIC BOOK SERVICES

NEW YORK • TORONTO • LONDON • AUCKLAND • SYDNEY • TOKYO

To Phillip
who started it all

Copyright © 1960 by Mildred Geiger Gilbertson.
Revised version copyright © 1979 by Mildred Geiger
Gilbertson. All rights reserved. This edition is pub-
lished by Scholastic Book Services, a division of
Scholastic Magazines, Inc., 50 West 44th Street, New
York, N.Y. 10036, by arrangement with Harper &
Row, Publishers, Inc.

12 11 10 9 8 7 6 5 4 3 2   9/7 0 1 2 3 4/8

Champions
Don't Cry

1

SALLY SAID DREAMILY, "Today I am a champion."

The words had a heavenly ring to them, and Sally rolled them slowly off her tongue as she repeated aloud, "Today I am a champion."

"Today you are nuts!" Dennis snorted, flopping onto the grass beside her. "Champion! Hah!"

Sally raised up on one elbow and studied her brother coldly. Brothers could be very tiresome sometimes, especially when they were two years older and took advantage of the fact.

"You're just jealous," Sally told him, "because *you* lost."

"Jealous!" Denny's voice cracked with indignation. "You think I'd *want* to win a cup if I only had to beat a poor old lady and a baby

1

in rompers to get it? Champion!" he finished with scorn. "You can't even spell it, let alone understand what it means."

"I can too," Sally retorted, but the words came out feebly. Somehow the bright splendor was fading from her day. She looked down at the little cup in her hand . . . the shining little cup that read "Fairfield Tennis Meet — Girls' Singles" . . . and already some of its glow had dulled.

That's Denny for you, Sally thought, always taking the glow off things. Defiantly she polished the cup on her sweater.

"I would have won it anyway," she muttered, "even if there *had* been a lot better players to beat."

Dennis said airily, "Talk . . . talk."

"Well, I could have, Dennis Barrett! I've got a good game — Mr. Cochran says so, and *he* ought to know."

Mr. Cochran, in his college years, had played Number One on his university tennis team. His words were tennis law to the young Barretts, whose games he had been building up, stroke by stroke, through two summers of patient advice and practice.

"Well . . ." Dennis backed hastily away from any argument with Mr. Cochran's opinion. "Even if you've *got* a good game, you sure haven't used it yet. The way you poked 'em into the fence against Rooney this afternoon! Mr. Cochran never told you to drive like that."

Sally said darkly, "Aw . . . that Isabel Rooney. She makes me mad."

"Something's always making you mad. You go off like a firecracker every time you lose a point." Dennis unscrambled himself and got to his feet. He stretched hugely. "That's why you better stay home from the *big* tournaments," he tossed back at her as he sauntered off.

Sally stared gloomily across the tennis courts. This afternoon, when she'd been winning that final game, she'd felt like — like — a tennis great with glossy green turf under her feet, and seats packed with cheering thousands. Now the courts were just dirt again, rough and weedy, with nets that sagged like Sally's spirits. Dennis was right: You had to win something bigger than a little old country-town tournament to be a champion.

But she *could* win something bigger, Sally thought stubbornly; just give her a chance and she'd show Denny! If only a big tournament would come along . . .

Big tournament! What had Denny said about big tournaments?

Sally sprang to her feet. "Dennis!" she

shouted, sprinting after him. "Dennis, what'd you say about a tournament? Are you going to one, Denny? Are you, honest? Oh, Denny, will you take me?"

"Hey, cut it out!" Denny protested. "Quit hangin' on me, will you?"

"But, Denny, you said —— "

"Well, if you'll be quiet long enough, I'll tell you. It's over in Maryville, two weeks from now. A district tournament, the paper said; that's bigger than just a city meet, and there'll be Junior divisions, instead of just Men's and Girls' like here. Mr. Cochran thought it'd be good practice for me to take it in."

"And me, Denny? Did he say it'd be good for me, too? Am I going?"

Dennis said, "Look, you ever heard of a thing called money? All tournaments aren't for free like this little old Fairfield one. There's an entry fee in a district meet — three dollars an event, the announcement said."

Sally swallowed hard. "I've got three dollars," she said, her voice very small. Three dollars represented two weeks' allowance; it was all her spending money for ice cream and movies and swims at the city pool.

"Yeh? And how'd you figure to get to Maryville? Walk?"

Maryville was twenty-five miles away . . . twenty-five hundred, it might as well be, if Sally had to produce bus fare too. Her voice was still smaller when she answered, "Okay. I'll walk."

Dennis snorted, but admitted grudgingly, "You sure have got the bug. Now if you only had a game ——— "

Sally swung on him, but it was just a gesture. She couldn't be really angry at anybody on this exciting day. Imagine it — she'd not only won a city championship (even if the city was just Fairfield, Iowa, population two thousand), but she was going to a district tournament! Yes, she was — even if she had to walk every step of the way.

2

AS FAR BACK as Sally's discovery that tennis was a real game, not just batting a ball against the house, she had dreamed of being a champion.

People admired champions, stared at them with respect, pointed them out. "That's Sally Barrett," they'd say. "You know — the tennis champion."

Why, even Miss Dickerson would have to admit she'd been wrong when Sally Barrett became a champion!

Miss Dickerson. At the thought of her Junior High principal, from whom she'd parted temporarily and without regret this June, Sally made a wry face.

But why spoil a lovely sunny day thinking of Miss Dickerson? It was the afternoon following the Fairfield tournament, and none too soon to start practicing seriously for the district meet in Maryville.

Sally caught up her racket and balls and ran out on the front porch, where Dennis lay comfortably in the swing.

"Denny," Sally coaxed, "let's play tennis, huh? Please, Denny?"

The swing swayed back and forth in a slow, maddening rhythm. Dennis gave a fair imitation of a boy gone totally deaf.

"Denny," Sally begged again, "*will* you play tennis with me?" She poked the swing with her racket to upset its calm motion.

Dennis roused himself to speech. "Nope."

"Dennis Barrett! Why not? You've got your tennis shoes on."

"Gonna play with the guys."

"I can give you a better game than any of them, Denny. You *know* I can."

"Look who's talking!"

"Well, I can! I won a cup yesterday, didn't I? Even if the competition wasn't much, that makes me — well, *practically* a champion."

"Practically off your rocker, you mean."

"You look here, Dennis Barrett, Mr. Cochran says —— "

"Oh, for Pete's sake, Mr. Cochran says, Mr. Cochran says! All he ever said was you've got pretty good strokes."

"Well, isn't that enough? If I've got the strokes, what else do I need?"

"Go away," Dennis begged, rolling over with his back to her. "Children don't interest me."

Sally pulled back her arm for a deadly whack at him, but consideration for her racket, not Dennis, stopped her. It was her only racket, and no longer new. The strings were frayed. If their tension hadn't loosened so much, they would surely have popped by now under some of the mighty drives Sally poured across the net.

When Sally practiced at the courts, passers-by stopped and stared in amazement. At thirteen, Sally was small for her age, and her twin blond ponytails made her look even younger. But with the force that she put into those forehand drives, Sally had some justification for her hope of becoming a real champion.

Now, Sally gave her brother up as a lost cause and went out into the yard to practice against the one opponent who was always ready to take her on — the house. *Pow, pow, pow,* her ball hit the smooth stretch of wall between the high-set dining-room window and the ornamental course of brick that jutted out just three feet above the ground.

Sally remembered the day, years ago, when she'd first discovered this fascinating game. She'd found an old racket and a can of balls in the hall closet and immediately wanted to play with them.

"All right," her mother had said, "but let's learn to do it right."

So she had brought Sally out to this same spot and showed her the right way to hit a tennis ball — standing sideways to the house, holding the racket as though shaking hands with it, stroking with her full arm in a smooth half-circle that followed through after the ball left the racket. Sally was never bored another summer day. Nothing but a really violent thunderstorm could keep her from her favorite game.

Those first balls had been pretty dead. To get them to bounce at all, Sally had developed a mighty swing. Later, when her father brought home an occasional, fuzzy new ball for her, Sally was able to back up thirty feet and more from the house and still have the ball bounce back to her. Her swing grew stronger; the muscles in her right arm were as hard as Denny's.

Then, two years ago, Denny got a racket and began to learn the real game of tennis from the caretaker at the courts. Sally just had to learn, too. Endlessly she teased and coaxed and badgered her brother till at last he gave up and took her to the courts.

"Now, look," he explained patiently, "first point, you serve to my right-hand service court; that's this square here by the net. It's got to land inside these lines, see? Then, next point, you serve to this left-hand square. Hey, now, wait a minute, when you serve you toss the ball up in the air and hit it above your head."

"I like my way better," said Sally, dropping the ball behind the baseline and swatting it over the net with a low swishing drive. The ball landed in the correct service court. Sally jumped up and down in glee, her ponytails flopping. "My point! My point!"

"It is not your point because I didn't even try to hit it," Dennis said in disgust. "That isn't the right way to serve."

"Why isn't it? It worked, didn't it?"

In the end Dennis gave up trying to teach her a service. He gave up teaching her a backhand, too; Sally, who had used only a forehand shot against the house, simply ran around the ball when it came to her left and returned it with that long, looping, whistling drive that was so deadly. Sally's brick wall had paid great dividends; by learning to

10

place her balls accurately between the window and the row of ornamental brick, she had developed a drive that just cleared the net and landed only inches within the baseline.

"My point! My point!" she shrilled, passing the ball past Denny's reaching racket time and again.

"Aw, nuts!" Dennis said at last, resigning his thankless job as coach. "You won't learn the rules, you won't learn any strokes you don't already know—all you want to do is win."

"Sure, why not?" Sally asked in surprise. "You're just mad because I beat you."

"You did not beat me! You can't beat a person when you don't even play the game right. I'm through."

But though Dennis stalked off the court, leaving her sputtering and weeping, Sally's tennis career had only just begun. An amused and interested young man who'd been watching the tennis lesson strolled over to Sally and said, "Here, hit me a few."

It was Sally's first introduction to Mr. Cochran, and the beginning of the coaching that he had, with increasing interest, given both Barretts ever since.

His praise of them was rare. Mostly Sally

and Dennis could judge their improving skill only by the fact that he continued to coach them. Under his stern gray eyes even Sally shut up and obediently learned to toss a ball in the air and serve it overhand. It was a harder job to remember not to run around her backhand, but for Mr. Cochran she at least tried.

"You can't build a solid house on weak foundations," he told her. "Every player has some strokes he's better at than others, but he won't be a champion till he's good at all of them."

Champion! Sally's eyes had lighted at the gallant word. "How soon will I be a champion?" she'd demanded.

Mr. Cochran's eyes held a faint twinkle. "I'll let you know as soon as it happens," he promised.

Remembering that promise, Sally sighed a little. She'd been so sure that yesterday was the day. But when Mr. Cochran had presented her with the cup, he'd said nothing but "Congratulations." He'd hardly even smiled. So Sally guessed she wasn't a champion *yet*. But maybe if she won the district tournament —

Sally's spirits soared. *Splat, pow,* the ball hit the bricks and rebounded clean and straight and hard. *Ping*, it sang as it connected with her racket strings.

To Sally there was music in the sound and the echo of a magic word.

Champion.

3 ═══

BICYCLE TIRES SQUEALED to a stop at the gate. "Gee, Sally, don't you *ever* lay down that racket?"

"Forty-one, forty-two . . . hi, Floppy . . . forty-three, forty-four . . ."

Floppy Merriam dropped to the grass, safely out of the way, and watched the ball, her dark head turning patiently from left to right. "What's your record — still fifty-two? Golly, I don't see how you do it. I can't hit it more than three times without missing." Floppy sighed hugely. "I think maybe I don't play well because I'm so heavy."

Sally frowned in concentration. "Forty-six, forty-seven."

"I don't know why I keep gaining this way. Maybe it's glands." Floppy pinched a fold of her waistline between thumb and forefinger. "Just look at that!"

Sally looked and missed the ball. Disgustedly she flung her racket after it. "Now look what you made me do! And I was up to forty-nine." She dropped down in a limp heap beside Floppy. "What's the matter with your waist?"

"It's enormous!" wailed Floppy. "Mother measured me for my new dress this afternoon, and it was *thirty inches*!"

"It's probably glands," Sally consoled her, "and pretty soon your doctor will realize it and give you pills and it'll just melt away." Sally wasn't quite sure she believed this myth herself, but she knew it was Floppy's dearest dream. "Anyway, your skin is just lovely."

"Yours would be just as pretty," Floppy said loyally, "if it weren't so tanned. You can't tell exactly what it does look like."

Sally rolled over on her back and stared at a passing cloud. "I don't care. Tennis champions are always brown as burnt toast. . . . What'll we do?"

Floppy considered. "Has your mother baked any fresh cookies? We could make a pitcher of grapeade —— "

"Mom hasn't baked this week. She's been too busy down at the shop, doing Dad's bookkeeping." Sally's frown returned. "I don't know why — it's not income-tax time or anything, but she's been down there every single day since school let out."

"Well — we could go down to the drug-store and get a sundae. I've some money."

"I haven't." Sally sat up abruptly. "I never have *any* money, and now with this tourna-ment coming—— I wish the folks would give me a bigger allowance."

"Why don't you do what I did? Remember how I made out a budget, and kept track of what I spent, and just *proved* how much more I needed? And my folks were so im-pressed, they gave me a clothes allowance, too. I've *really* been rolling since then."

"Well, sure, because you haven't bought any clothes. But I don't think that would work with my family. Dad's awfully strong-minded when it comes to saying no. Like not letting me stay out late on baby-sitting jobs . . . and if you have to be home by ten o'clock, who *wants* you to baby-sit? I can't even make enough to buy my tennis balls."

"I know, it's awful," Floppy sympathized. "I tell you what — the sundaes will be my treat."

Sally hesitated, but finally shook her head. "Thanks, but I guess I shouldn't. Mr. Coch-ran says too much sweet stuff cuts your wind."

"Well, all right, then, let's go see what's in your refrigerator."

"Okay." Sally brushed the grass from her faded blue denim shorts. "We can make some grapeade anyway."

The Barrett kitchen was always an inviting place. Usually there was a jar of fresh cookies, crackly with nuts or chewy with raisins. Or a loaf of nut bread that needn't be saved for mealtime. But this week Mrs. Barrett hadn't had time to bake a thing. What was going on in the car-repair business that Dad should need her so much, Sally wondered.

There was some of last night's roast in the refrigerator. Sally cut two generous slices and began making sandwiches, while Floppy mixed orange and grape juice in a big pitcher.

"Gorgeous!" she sighed, stirring and tasting. "Only I think it needs a little more sugar."

"Not in mine," Sally warned. "That orange juice makes it plenty sweet."

"Well, it doesn't need *much*," Floppy adful. "Did you ever have your conference with Miss Dickerson, Sally? You put it off so long, mitted, adding three sugar cubes to her glass- I thought maybe you'd get out of it."

Sally scowled. She slapped lettuce into the sandwiches with a force that sent crumbs flying. "I talked to her," she said shortly. "Let's take these out on the back steps, shall we?"

"What did she say? She gave *me* an awful talking-to ... told me I should be an all-round good sport and enter more into activities if I wanted to make my school years memorable. I said I didn't like games much, and she said they were valuable friendship-makers and would repay the energy I put into them a thousandfold." Floppy sighed deeply and took a big bite of sandwich. "I don't think she just had friendship-making in mind, either; she looked at my waistline too often."

"She's touched," Sally said darkly, tapping her head.

"What did she tell you?" Floppy persisted.

"Pour me another glass of grapeade," Sally stalled.

Ice tinkled musically as Floppy poured. The sound brought Dennis from the front porch. "Hey, what are you kids doing? Eating everything in the house? How about something for me?"

Ordinarily Sally would have told him to

look after himself, but now she jumped to her feet hastily. "Do you want a sandwich, Denny? I'll make you one."

"Well, that's more like it," said Dennis happily, pouring himself a tall glass of grape-ade. "Make me two, while you're at it."

"Okay," said Sally meekly.

Dennis looked startled, then suspicious. He inspected the sandwiches carefully when Sally brought them, looking for a heavy sprinkling of dry mustard or pepper. But the sandwiches looked good and tasted better. Dennis relaxed.

"I guess I won't bother calling any of the guys," he said amiably. "You'll do all right for practice today; I want to take it easy anyway."

Even that insult didn't strike a spark from Sally, so anxious was she to keep the conversation from Miss Dickerson. "Swell! I'll get my racket. You don't mind, do you, Floppy?"

"Nope," agreed Floppy, stuffing in the last of her sandwich. "I'll go get my racket, too."

Dennis made a horrible face, but Sally, with quick loyalty, said, "Okay, you do that. We'll get in a game later on."

"Good grief," Dennis moaned as Floppy

bicycled off, "that's not tennis she plays. It's annie-annie-over with a racket. How can you stand it?"

"You just hush, Dennis Barrett! Floppy's my friend."

"So what? That doesn't make her a tennis player."

"Well, she *thinks* it's tennis. And anyway we have *fun*."

Dennis shook his head. "Girls," he said. "Well, come on — champ!" He roared at his own joke. "Or a reasonable facsimile, that is!"

4

THE TENNIS COURTS in Fairfield were only
dirt, but Mr. Cochran said a little town like
theirs was lucky to have any courts at all.

In the spring all the tennis players got out
and weeded every evening till the two courts
were in good shape. Then in June a caretaker
hired by the city took charge and kept up
the weeding and rolling, the marking of clean
white lines fresh each morning.

"Don't know why we can't just let the
weeds grow, and mow 'em close," the pres-
ent caretaker, who was no tennis player,
grumbled. "Pictures I've seen of tennis
courts, plenty of 'em, show green all over.
Even that Wimbledon."

"That's turf, not weeds," Mr. Cochran explained to him. "Special turf that hugs the
ground so closely it's a perfect surface for
bouncing balls. Weeds make bumps; even or-

dinary grass does. The ball would take a crooked bounce."

"So who cares?" demanded the caretaker. "Put a little more fun into the game, not knowing where the ball's going to bounce."

But he went on weeding the courts in spite of his personal opinion.

Both courts were open when Dennis and Sally arrived. The sun was high and hot; most players preferred to wait till later in the afternoon, but the Barretts liked the heat.

Dennis measured the net at the center, tightened it a bit at the net post. Sally toed the baseline impatiently.

"Ready?" she called.

"Of course I'm not ready." Dennis frowned. "We haven't even warmed up. Don't you know better than to start serving cold?"

"Who's cold?" scoffed Sally, but she gave him a long, slow, underhand ball instead of a service. "Ninety in the shade, and he's cold!" she called over her shoulder to Floppy, who was parking her bike outside the fence.

Floppy laughed obligingly. Floppy always thought Sally's jokes superbly funny. But Dennis didn't.

"You know blamed well what I mean," he said. "Do you want to get laid up all summer with tennis elbow because you charge in and serve too hard too quickly?"

Sally suspected he was right. He almost always was, because he read tennis books and talked long, serious hours with Mr. Cochran. So she pinged the ball back and forth leisurely till Denny declared himself ready to begin a set.

Once real play started, Sally's leisureliness vanished. She half crouched at the baseline, awaiting Denny's serve, blocking it when it was too hard, returning it with zip and power when she could.

And when the ball came to her left, invariably Sally ran around it and whacked it with her strong forehand.

With the games three up, Dennis caught the ball and said disgustedly, "Where's your backhand?"

"What do you mean, where's my backhand? That was my point, Dennis Barrett! You didn't even try to hit the ball."

"I don't care whose point it is. You aren't out here to win a match —— "

"I am, too!" Sally declared.

"You are here to practice. How can you learn anything if you try to win all the time?"

"You're just scared you'll get beat."

Dennis set his lips hard. "I don't care *who* beats who. If you try to win every point, you never use your weaker strokes. Mr. Cochran says you shouldn't even keep score when you're practicing."

"We-ell . . ." As always, when Mr. Cochran was quoted, Sally backed down. "Okay. Thirty all."

The game went to deuce and stayed there. Neither one could win two points in a row to run it out. Sally was trying very hard to use the right stroke at the right place, but the next time she got advantage point, she just couldn't help herself. When Dennis put his return to her backhand, Sally ran nimbly around the ball and whacked it with her deadly short cross-court forehand. It just cleared the net and ticked chalk off Denny's service line as it swished past him for point and game.

Floppy applauded loudly. "Gée, Sally, that was fabulous!"

Sally looked sidelong at Dennis. It was obvious he didn't share Floppy's opinion. He looked angry enough to bite a chunk out of his racket.

"Well, what's wrong with you?" she asked defensively. "It was a good shot. It won me the game, didn't it?"

Dennis said in disgust, "Look, I gave you a soft ball on purpose. I didn't want to pound your backhand when you were just practicing."

"Oh, you're just saying that," Sally said uncertainly. "And anyway I don't *want* you giving me anything."

"Okay. Just try and get another point!"

Denny's confidence made Sally nervous. She served cautiously. Her first ball hit the net cord; her second ball was softer and even more careful. Dennis returned it with a vicious chop. Now Sally knew what his strategy was to be.

"Oh, Denny," she wailed, leaping a fraction too late for the ball, "you *know* I hate chops!"

Chopping, or undercutting, a ball almost always caught Sally off balance; it was something her brick wall hadn't prepared her for. An undercut ball had a lower bounce, and it bounced straight up — or even backwards toward the net — instead of toward her. Worst of all, if she tried to return a chopped ball with her favorite top-spin drive, she'd very likely plop it into the net. It had to be *lifted* back with another chop or a lob, and Sally liked neither stroke; they were dull and slow compared to a good hard drive.

Impatiently, though, she tried first one stroke, then the other. But sooner or later she'd get exasperated and whack one of Denny's infuriating chops with a flat drive. Into the net it would go. Another point lost. Dennis ran out the set six games to four.

"That wasn't fair," Sally protested.

"Why wasn't it? You think everybody's gonna set the ball up for you so you can show off your drive?" Dennis looked well pleased with himself.

"It takes all the fun out of the game," Sally grumbled.

"Well, you have to learn how to beat a chop, not just go on playing your own game and getting angry because you don't win."

From the bench Floppy spoke up indignantly. "I bet you were just scared to hit 'em the right way, for fear she'd beat you."

"Oh, for Pete's sake!" Dennis slung his racket over his shoulder and stalked off to the bangboard at the far end of the courts.

Floppy repeated stubbornly, "Well, I'll bet he was. If you've got a stroke that's good, why shouldn't you use it? It's silly not to. I'll bet you could beat almost any girl in the state with that forehand drive of yours; it's just tremendous."

Floppy's loyalty was heart-warming.

Though Sally wouldn't admit it for the world, it was sometimes pretty nice to know that Floppy thought her wonderful. Sally's spirits bounced back to normal.

"Okay, let's see if it'll beat you," she invited.

"Me?" Floppy cried. "You could beat me with a — a dishpan for a racket! But all right." She took her place at the baseline. "Serve 'em up."

5

FLOPPY'S TENNIS GAME was, to put it mildly, simply awful. She held her racket like a fly-swatter, looped up balls in weak uncertain lobs, took wild swings that missed the ball entirely, and performed gyrations that would have done credit to an acrobat. She screamed when she saw the ball coming, and squealed when she missed.

By the time they'd played two games, Sally was weak with laughter. Floppy was so funny she couldn't help it. Fortunately, Floppy knew it, too, and didn't mind the laughter.

"Not so hard!" she begged as the ball came floating toward her. She ducked, twisted, crouched, took a wild overhand pass at the ball and punched it into the net.

"I *can't* put them over any softer than that," Sally giggled.

But she tried. She fed Floppy very, very gentle balls placed where Floppy wouldn't have to move a step to hit them. And every now and then she got to laughing so hard that she popped up her own balls in ridiculous arcs.

So noisy was their game that Sally didn't hear Mr. Cochran's car pull into the parking area. Nor did she see his tall, lean figure with the powerful shoulders till he crossed behind Floppy's baseline. Then she caught the ball quickly.

"Hello, Mr. Cochran," she called.

He gave her a brief nod and continued across courts to the bangboard, where Denny was practicing. "Good boy," he said. "Want to hit me a few?"

Not a word to Sally. Not a word. Sally felt hot color flooding her face. Oh, dear, why had he come when she was acting so silly? She hated to have him see her play anything but her very best game.

"I guess — maybe we'd better stop now, Floppy," she said.

Floppy cried, "I should hope so! I'm really tired; I'll bet I lost five pounds. Well, guess I'll stick around and watch you play Mr. Cochran."

She dropped onto the bench, fanning herself. Sally joined her, carefully pulling her sweater around her shoulders, as Mr. Cochran had taught her, to avoid the sudden cooling off that could cause cramp.

"Put your sweater on," she murmured to Floppy.

"On a day like this?" Floppy asked loudly. "Do you think I'm nuts? Hey, let's get a drink. I could swallow a barrelful."

And she practically did, Sally thought. In her turn, Sally took only a small mouthful of water, rinsed her mouth, and spat it out. "I'm trying to get used to not drinking when I play," she explained to Floppy. "You can get waterlogged awfully easily during a match, even sick."

They went back to the bench and watched Mr. Cochran and Dennis exchange long drives, forehand and backhand. Sally never got over her wondering admiration of Mr. Cochran's strokes. She could see why he'd been Number One on his university tennis team, but she *didn't* see why he wasn't Number One in the whole country. How could anyone be better?

"You just haven't seen enough good tennis yet," Mr. Cochran had told her. "It's a long, long climb to the top."

Dennis was playing well, too, Sally had to

admit. He was a plugger; his strokes hadn't come naturally, as Sally's had. He'd had to set his jaw and get in there and work for every bit of the skill he now showed. Watching him, Sally realized in surprise how much better he was this summer than last. They'd played almost evenly then; now he was pulling steadily ahead of her. Sally didn't like that.

She didn't like Mr. Cochran not speaking to her either. It made her a little scared. What had she done now? Mr. Cochran never did say much — his few words of praise were like rain in the desert — but when he was displeased, he said nothing at all.

"Hey, aren't you ever going to play?" Floppy asked at last, bored with waiting.

"Maybe you'd better go on home," Sally said. She wanted to go herself, but she felt she had to stay until Mr. Cochran said whatever he was going to say. "You go along and I'll call you later."

"Well, okay." Floppy strolled over to her bike. "You want to play again tomorrow?" she called back. "That sure was fun."

"I'll see," said Sally, very low.

"What did you say?"

"I said — I guess I'll be practicing pretty hard for the tournament all week. But I'll call you, Floppy."

"Yes, you do that." Floppy's voice, drifting back, sounded a little offended. "Providing I'm home, of course — I expect I'm going to be pretty busy this week myself."

Sally was almost in tears. She'd hurt Floppy's feelings, and she was somehow in disgrace with Mr. Cochran. Even Dennis was mad at her. Oh, dear, was being a champion worth it?

6 ——

MR. COCHRAN FINISHED a long rally with Dennis, caught the ball and came over to Sally.

"Want a workout?" he asked.

"Oh, yes!" cried Sally, jumping to her feet, enormously relieved at his noticing her at last.

It *was* a workout, too. For half an hour Mr. Cochran pounded Sally's weak points unmercifully. Sally, longing to earn his praise with superb forehand drives, found herself struggling with backhands and half-volleys and services, retrieving despised chops, running from baseline to net, from left court to right, till her tongue hung out.

"Good enough," Mr. Cochran said at the end. "A session like *that* every day, and you'll be ready for Maryville."

There had been just a slight extra emphasis on his "that." Sally knew he was thinking of the exhibition she'd been putting on with Floppy when he came, and she blushed.

"I don't play with Floppy often," she murmured.

"You shouldn't at all," Mr. Cochran said. He explained patiently, "When you play against a much weaker player, you hurt your own game. You hit soft shots, and let too many balls get by you. Then when you want to play well, you find that your reactions are slower and your strokes aren't in the groove. You can't afford that, Sally, if you're going to be a tournament player."

"But Floppy's my best friend!" Sally cried. "And she loves to play."

Mr. Cochran turned toward his car. "It's your choice, Sally," he said. "I've told you all along that being a champion isn't easy. This is one of the hard parts."

Sally bicycled home very slowly, letting Dennis go on ahead. What could she say the next time Floppy wanted to play tennis? It wouldn't be fair just to fib and stall.

This champion business — was there more to it than Sally had thought? More than just having good strokes?

Mom was home when Sally arrived, and the kitchen was spicy-sweet with the scent of fresh apple pie. Sally's spirits perked up.

"Hi, Mom — mmm, that smells good!"

"You're just hungry." Her mother smiled. "Have a good game?"

"Well, I *guess* so. Anyway, Mr. Cochran said 'good enough' when we finished practicing. That means an awful lot, coming from him."

"I'm sure of it. If he ever says 'splendid,' you'll be ready for Wimbledon." When Mrs. Barrett's eyes crinkled with laughter, she looked surprisingly like an older, darker edition of Sally. Without the ponytails, of course. Mrs. Barrett's long hair was pinned in braids around her head.

Sally was always surprised to notice how brown the braids showed against the graying hair in front. It was hard to think of Mom as a youngster whose hair was as dark as that all over, a little girl who wore pigtails and played games and had secrets. And got mad?

No, thought Sally with a sigh, she didn't think Mom had ever lost her temper. She was too patient now, and good-natured. Sally guessed *she* was the only girl since creation who got mad so very quickly. Maybe there *had* been a little bit of truth in what Miss Dickerson had said — only a very small speck, of course. Mostly Miss Dickerson had been horribly unfair and not a bit understanding. Sally put her out of her mind quickly.

"Hey, Mom, what am I going to do about clothes for the tournament? I don't have a tennis dress."

Mrs. Barrett took the pie from the oven before she answered. Then she said slowly, "How much is this tournament going to cost, Sally?"

Sally was suddenly very still. The way Mom said that — were her parents worried about money? Was that why Mom spent so much time at the shop, working on the ledgers that showed expenses and income? Maybe that's why they hadn't given Sally the bigger allowance she'd hoped to have this summer.

"Mom, can't we afford a tennis dress for me?" she asked anxiously.

Mrs. Barrett turned from the stove, laughter erasing her faint worried frown. "Goodness, you look as though we're down to three grains of corn and you'll never be queen of the May! I'm sure we can manage the dress. But what else do you need?"

"Not a thing," Sally said stoutly. She had wanted to mention bus fare, but now she hoped her mother wouldn't think of it. Something must be very wrong for Mom to hesitate over the cost of a tennis dress. The Barretts were far from rich, but money had never been *that* tight. Sally gave her mother a hard hug. "Thanks. Do you need some help on dinner? Shall I make the salad, huh? And peel the potatoes?"

Mrs. Barrett said, smiling, "If I could only afford new tennis clothes for you *every* day! I hope some of this industry lasts over till dusting's done tomorrow."

Sally made a face. She hated cleaning day. Washing day was fun; ironing day wasn't bad. Baking day was most fun of all. But cleaning day ——

The next morning, however, dusting and dust-mopping and bathroom-cleaning went fast and painlessly. For one thing, it was raining, so tennis was out of the question even if she'd been free to play. For another, her mind wasn't on the hated cleaning but on the coming tournament. Excitement about it built up in her mind till she felt like a balloon about to burst.

She pictured the great day in her mind — arriving at the strange courts, sitting on a bench to wait for her match to be called, getting up to meet her first opponent.

But with that scene the pictures broke off

and Sally felt a small cold shiver start up her spine. This wouldn't be like the Fairfield tournament, where there had only been four entries in Sally's division and she'd known them all for years. The girl she played at Maryville would be a stranger, maybe years older and terribly good. What if Sally couldn't even return her balls? What if she just stumbled around after them, looking foolish, while Dennis died of embarrassment for her?

By now Sally had scared herself so badly she was cold to her fingertips.

She put away the scouring powder and brush she'd used on the tub, gathered up the soiled towels, and hung out fresh ones. This was her last cleaning job. She was free now, but with the rain still streaming down the windows, what was there to do?

"I'll call Flop," she decided quickly. Flop never stayed mad long. They'd figure out something to do that would erase the coming tournament entirely from Sally's mind.

The telephone sat on a little table under the stairs. Sally came halfway downstairs, reached for the phone through the railing, and settled herself comfortably over half a dozen steps.

Bz-z-z-z went the busy signal when she dialed the Merriam number.

Sally sighed. "If that's Flop on the phone, it could be busy for hours."

She could hear a murmur of voices in the living room, one of them her mother's. The door was almost closed. Who had come? Sally hadn't heard the doorbell.

She dialed again. It hadn't been Flop on the phone after all, for it was Mrs. Merriam who answered and she said Flop wasn't home.

"I sent her downtown to buy herself some underwear," Mrs. Merriam explained. "The ones she's been wearing are a disgrace; I simply refuse to repair them any longer. Since we put Flop on a clothes allowance, she's become simply *stingy* about replacing things that don't show so much, you know. New dresses, that's a different story, but she thinks she can put them on over *rags!*"

Sally felt that Flop came by her long, wordy telephone habits naturally. "Okay, Mrs. Merriam," she put in as soon as she politely could. "You tell her I'll call later, will you?"

She was reaching through the railing to replace the phone when she realized that the second voice in the living room was Dad's! Why, what was he doing home in the morning?

She heard him say "mighty short of

money, though . . ." and her mother's confident answer, "We'll manage all right, Dave." Then Dad said something about "the bank" and "not liking debt" before Sally realized she was practically eavesdropping.

Puzzled, reluctant, she went slowly back upstairs to her room. What *was* wrong at the shop?

7 ======

KIDS WERE ALWAYS crying about "being broke." They'd say, "Lend me a dime, will you?" Or, when they walked past the drugstore, "Hey, don't slow down — I couldn't buy a milk shake if they were two for a nickel!"

But that was kids. It was different and sort of frightening for grownups to be short of money. Especially parents. What did their families do?

Sally began cleaning out her closet. This was a twice-a-year job that she usually put off till the Salvation Army truck was practically at the door to pick up discards. But now Sally felt the need to keep busy. Steadily she worked her way through dresses and old jeans and skirts and blouses, trying on some to see if she'd outgrown them, putting quite a few things back on the rack that usually she'd have been glad to give away. Sally didn't come right out and put it into words, but in her mind was a little worry that maybe Dad couldn't afford new clothes this summer to replace them.

She heard her parents' voices in the hall, then the sound of the screen door closing and Dad's pick-up starting. A little later Denny's bike screeched to a halt in the driveway and fell over with a clatter. Minutes after that, Mom called upstairs, "Sally! Lunch is ready."

"Where's Dad?" asked Dennis, looking at the table set for three.

"He won't be home for lunch," Mrs. Barrett said, ladling out soup. "He's talking to some men from the bank this noon."

The soup was Sally's favorite — chicken vegetable — but suddenly it tasted like nothing but hot water. She refused seconds, and began clearing the table silently.

Mom disappeared upstairs and came down in a fresh dress. "I'll be at the shop till dinnertime, dear," she told Sally. "You might start the potatoes at five thirty."

"Okay," said Sally. But as she watched her mother back the car out of the driveway and start for town, all the worries that had been scuttling around her mind like mice suddenly formed into words.

"Denny," she burst out, "what's wrong at the shop? Are we — have we run out of money?"

Dennis, stuffing an apple into his pocket as he made for the porch swing, said, "Huh? Now what goofy idea you got in your head?"

Sally followed him to the porch and sat on the top step, her chin propped on her fists. "Well, maybe you haven't noticed, but Mom's been at the shop practically every day since school let out. She never used to be, Denny. And — and this morning Dad was home. I heard them talking in the living room when I was phoning. He said something about the bank and debts and being short of money, and Mom said we'd manage all right. I'm scared, Denny."

"You're nuts," Denny said, but he didn't sound as positive about it as he usually did. In fact, he looked faintly uneasy.

"I *have* heard them talking at night," he admitted at last. "Nothing they said, just their voices sounding kind of serious."

"Oh, Denny, could Dad be going to lose the shop? What would we *do*?"

"Well, don't go off in a tizzy. That sure wouldn't help."

"But what would help?"

"Look, nobody's said they *need* help. But

if they did, I guess making some money of our own would be the best. Even if it's only our own spending money."

Sally looked tragic. "Money! I can't even make enough from baby-sitting to buy my tennis balls. And now there's the tournament coming, and I asked Mom for a new tennis dress —— "

"Stop borrowing trouble, for Pete's sake! Just because you were eavesdropping . . . Serves you right."

"I didn't eavesdrop, Dennis Barrett! I went upstairs just as quickly as I could so I wouldn't hear any more."

Dennis closed his book and swung his feet to the floor. He stared thoughtfully out over the porch railing. "Rain's stopped. Think I'll go downtown."

Sally looked at him suspiciously. "Where are you going?"

"Oh, just around. Maybe stop at the shop."

Sally got up abruptly. "I'll go along."

For once he didn't tell her to mind her own business. Sally wheeled her bike from the garage, and side by side they rode through the quiet rain-washed streets, skirting the deeper pools of water. That in itself showed they were bound on serious business; ordinarily they would have splashed right through the middle.

When they reached the Barrett auto-repair shop, with its sign of the swinging bear outside, they parked their bikes and strolled carelessly in. It wasn't a big shop. Except for Dad, only old Tim Feely worked there.

Right now both Dad and Tim were deep in a Chevrolet engine, their heads bent over their flashing trouble lights. Another car was up on the grease rack, and the two others waiting their turns seemed to fill the room to bursting.

"Sure aren't hurting for business," Dennis whispered over his shoulder.

Sally nodded. "But maybe people don't pay their bills," she suggested anxiously.

They didn't bother Dad, just called "Hi" and went on into the office. This was a little cubbyhole of a room. The big untidy rolltop desk reached almost from wall to wall. At a tall stool before an old-fashioned adding machine Mom was perched, her eyes and one finger on the long column of figures in the open book beside her. Wisps of gray-brown hair strayed out of her braid; every now and then she put up her pencil and absentmindedly thrust a strand back in.

"Hello, what are you two doing downtown?" she asked, looking up to see them in the doorway.

Denny said, "Oh, nothing." He wandered

over and lounged against the desk. Mom went on adding figures. When she reached the end of the column, she was frowning.

Denny asked, "What's the matter? Get the wrong answer?"

"I could have got a better one," she admitted, but the frown disappeared in a crinkle of laugh lines.

Dennis looked over her shoulder at the big book. "Is that stuff hard to do?"

"You mean, if it is, how come I can do it?" teased Mom. "You're *really* hard up for something to do if you're interested in bookkeeping. Want to take over my job?"

"Heck, no!" Denny hurriedly backed away. "You know what I got in math last year." He stirred the papers on the desk idly, and yawned. "Well . . . guess we'll push off. This darn rain —— "

"Oh, that's it! No tennis." Mom smiled. "Well, behave yourselves."

She turned another page and went on with her adding. Dennis signaled Sally, and they went back to their bicycles.

A block down the street, Dennis said, "I saw a couple of letters from the bank on the desk. They were in their envelopes, though."

"Could you make out anything from that book she was working on?"

"No-o. Except that those were all expenses she was adding . . . checks they'd paid out for stuff."

"All that!" cried Sally, aghast. "Oh, Denny!"

They pedaled in sober silence another two blocks. Then Dennis put on his brakes sharply before a grocery store. "You go on along. I'm going to stop here."

"I'll wait for you."

"I don't want you to."

"Why not?"

Dennis scuffed the sidewalk with his toe. "Because — maybe I'll be a while. Or maybe I'll be stopping other places. Somebody might need a delivery boy or something."

"Oh, Denny, you're going to get a job!"

"Well, maybe. If I'm lucky."

Sally said wistfully, "I wish there was something I could do. . . . Good luck, Denny." Soberly she turned toward home.

8 ═══════

NOW SALLY'S WORRIES were hopping around her mind like popcorn in a hot pan. Dennis hated summer jobs, except for early-morning ones like his paper route; they kept him from playing tennis. If he was actually out job-hunting, that meant he was as anxious about Mom and Dad as she was.

"But what can *I* do?" thought Sally in distress. "There must be something."

Well, there was. Maybe it didn't pay anything, but it was a help anyway. During these weeks while Mom was spending so much time at the shop, the housework never really got done. Mending was piled high; socks overflowed the darning basket; the cookie jar and cake pan remained empty.

"And some of it I could do," Sally told herself, "even if I *don't* like to."

She knew how to run a sewing machine (hadn't she made herself a skirt in home ec. last year?), so she could easily mend straight rips like a torn sheet. And darning — Sally could darn, but it was the kind of slow, patient work she hated.

Maybe Mom hated it, too, Sally thought, sorting her own socks from the darning basket and taking them out to the front steps to work on. Probably that's why she took the darning with her to Mrs. Merriam's or to church circle to do, where she could talk with somebody so busily she wouldn't notice what her hands were doing.

But Sally had no one to talk to; she had nothing at all to put her mind on but this slow weaving in and out of a tangly colored thread. She set her lips tight; her brows drew together in an impatient frown; she wriggled from one position to another on the hard concrete step.

Sunshine streamed through the last draggle of clouds and sparkled on the puddles. By tomorrow morning the courts would be dry enough to roll; she could get out and practice again.

Once more a picture of the coming tournament unrolled like a film in Sally's mind . . . right up to the moment when she toed the baseline and swung into her first serve. Then thought of the stranger across the net started that scared shiver up her spine.

Sally stabbed the needle into her finger and looked up with an exclamation to see someone pedaling slowly past the house. Very slowly. And very carefully not looking at Sally.

Why, it was Flop!

For the first time Sally remembered that Floppy hadn't phoned her back this morning as she usually would have. That meant she was still hurt about yesterday. Sally felt guilty.

"Hi," she called.

At the last possible moment Flop turned her head and seemed surprised to find herself passing the Barrett house. "Oh, hello," she said casually.

"Aren't you going to stop?"

"Stop? Why, no, it hadn't occurred to me," said Flop with great indifference.

A giggle stirred inside Sally. Flop was so very funny when she was haughty. But if Sally laughed now, she'd never be forgiven.

She coaxed, "Oh, come on, Flop, don't be mad."

"Who's mad?" Flop stared off into space, one toe on the ground, apparently ready to start off again any moment.

Sally rolled up a pair of socks and put them with the mended pile. "How we do run through socks!" she said, sounding very much like her mother. "Look at that stack still to do. Want to help?"

Curiosity overcame Flop's pose of indifference. "What're you doing? Darning? I never knew you darned."

"Well, I don't mostly. I mean I *should*, but — anyway, I thought I'd do mine today to help Mom. She's so rushed lately."

"Is she downtown again? She never stays home and bakes anymore, does she?" Flop asked wistfully. She wheeled her bike up the walk. "I'd help, but I don't know how."

"I guess I've done enough anyway," Sally decided, sucking her pricked finger. "I don't know why they make needles so sharp at both ends. I've about worn this finger out, pushing that stupid thing."

"My mother uses a thimble."

"So does mine. But when I put a thimble on my middle finger, then I push with my ring finger. I suppose I could put a thimble on *every* finger — but then I'd probably push it with my thumb. What've you been doing?"

"I had to go to the store for Mother. That's her cake flour in the basket."

"This street isn't on your way to the store."

"Well, I had to finish the potato chips I bought. Maybe Mother might not have wanted me to charge them."

"Mom won't let us charge things. We're supposed to pay cash out of our allowance."

"Well, I'm not exactly supposed to charge either. I mean, sometimes it's all right and sometimes it isn't. I didn't know which it would be today, so I just ate the potato chips first."

Flop sounded as if that made everything all right. Sally was glad Mom just laid down a rule and stuck to it; that way she always knew where she stood.

"You want to ride along while I take home the flour?" asked Flop.

"Okay."

Sally put away the darning and joined Floppy. They pedaled slowly down the street until Flop abruptly turned a corner.

"Hey, this isn't the way!" Sally cried, zigzagging wildly to make the turn in time.

"Oh, what's the hurry?" asked Flop.

She pedaled more and more slowly, humming a little tune and fluffing out her long black hair. Suddenly she smiled brilliantly and began an animated chatter with Sally that didn't make sense at all. Not till Sally spotted Jeff Donnelly out in his yard, shooting baskets at the hoop on his garage door.

Sally groaned aloud, but not till they were out of Jeff's hearing. "Honest, Flop, are you still mooning over *him?*"

Flop tossed her head. "I don't know what you're talking about."

"You do, too. Look at the number of times you've dragged me down this street! And he never notices anyway. You're just plain silly."

Flop came down hard on her pedals. "And you're just plain young, that's what's the matter with you!"

It was Sally's turn to be angry. Every now and then Floppy remembered that she was almost a full year older than Sally, and until she forgot it again, she treated Sally like a baby sister.

Indignantly now, Sally zipped into top speed, passing Flop with her head in the air. But Flop was already sorry. She came panting in Sally's wake.

"Don't be mad, Sally. Hey, slow down, will you? I'm getting an awful cramp. Sal-ly!"

Sally wouldn't look around, but she quit pedaling and coasted till Flop overtook her.

Flop cast about anxiously for a new subject that would keep the peace.

"Sally," she said eagerly, "you never did tell me what Miss Dickerson said to you. What was it, huh?"

9 ═══════

NOW IT WAS Sally who searched for another
subject, but there wasn't anything in the
whole long stretch of bare street to give her
an idea.

"Oh, nothing much," she called back airily.
"I bet your mother's in a hurry to get that
flour."

"No, she isn't. She probably won't use it
till dinnertime. Did Miss Dickerson give you
a big line on what it takes to get the most
from your school years?"

"Oh, sure, she said a lot of *words*," Sally
admitted crossly. "They didn't add up to anything. Let's get rid of the flour and go see
if the courts have dried."

Flop, dodging puddles, didn't bother to
answer this absurdity. She pedaled in silence
for half a block, then guessed wisely, "I'll

bet she said plenty about your quitting the *Widget*."

Sally pulled up at Flop's front steps and flung herself off her bicycle. Her dark blond eyebrows were drawn tight together in a frown. She dropped to the steps, elbows on knees, chin resting on two hard-balled fists.

"She gives me a pain," she muttered. "Anybody with *any* self-respect would have quit."

"She did talk about it, then. I knew she was mad when you quit. Did you tell her why you did?"

"Can you imagine telling Miss Dickerson anything?" Sally scowled. "She just steam-rollers along, crushing you to a pancake."

Sally stared angrily off across the Merriams' green lawn, seeing Miss Dickerson instead of the tall elm, remembering the words that seemed to her so unjust.

The *Widget* was the Junior High newspaper, and Sally had wanted to be on the staff more than anything except winning a tennis title. All year she had worked for the paper enthusiastically as a reporter, submitting news bits, suggesting columns, suffering a letdown every Friday when she saw so few of her offerings in the paper, but consoling herself with the thought that next year things would be different. She'd surely have a place on the staff then. Why, she might even be editor!

"That Bert Goodwin, why is he such a big deal?" Sally grumbled now. "He couldn't write a good story if you fed it to him word by word."

"He's awfully steady and reliable," Flop reminded her. "You can always trust him to get things done."

Sally burst out, "Oh, you make me sick! You don't have to sound exactly like Miss Dickerson."

It had been a blow to have a boy who — Sally knew positively — didn't have half her imagination and writing ability chosen as next year's editor; it had been even more dreadful to see one important staff position after another go to classmates who were only good steady toilers. Sally was listed, again, as just a reporter. To her that seemed the lowest of the low. Why, practically everybody who went out for the *Widget* was made a reporter, even the youngest and dumbest seventh-grader! So Sally had quit.

"It wasn't fair," she muttered. "You *know* I should have had a better place the second year. Wouldn't anybody be mad, getting passed up like that?"

Flop nodded gravely. "You really got the short end. It wasn't fair at all."

Her sympathy opened Sally's lips, and all her grievances poured out. "Miss Dickerson said I must learn to have patience, I must do the unrewarding work cheerfully," she mimicked the principal's precise tones. "Learn responsibility, and be reliable above all. As though it made any difference, those stupid assignments I didn't get in. Checking with the teachers on classwork, writing the list of next week's announcements. Nobody reads that stuff anyway."

No, it wasn't announcements and schedules that made kids grab for the *Widget* every Friday and stand around in giggling groups, reading it. It was the columns of fun-poking and the feature stories. Like the sample columns Sally had turned in hopefully throughout the year, sometimes working so hard on them she forgot to do the dull assignments she'd been given.

"Miss Dickerson said: 'Always remember stars are made, not born,'" Sally quoted grumpily. "'A star is the total of years spent as understudy and bit player and second lead.' Now, whatever has that got to do with a *newspaper?*"

"She's touched, I guess," Flop said comfortingly. "Been there too long, maybe. I'd just forget about her."

But it was hard to forget so imposing a figure as Miss Dickerson. When she talked, she sounded a little like a minister, so confident that she knew what she was saying even when, like this, it hadn't made a bit of sense.

"Miss Dickerson said," Sally repeated glumly, "that my tendency is to rush enthusiastically into every activity, then give it up as soon as I find there's hard, dull work involved. She says I have lots of energy and talent, but no staying power. Did you ever hear anything more mean? I just hate her."

"So do I," Flop declared loyally. "But don't you worry, she's just completely bats. Look at your tennis game — I guess it takes plenty of work to learn to play like that."

Sally was comforted by the reminder. She guessed that when she was a tennis champion, even Miss Dickerson would have to admit she had staying power.

"I'll show her," Sally declared.

"Sure you will," Flop said, "the sourball! . . . Come on, let's go see if Mother's baked any cookies."

10 —————

THERE WERE NO cookies, but Mrs. Merriam
was waiting impatiently to mix a cake.

"I thought you'd had to mill the flour yourself," she said, taking the box from Flop.
"Where on earth have you been? Hello, Sally.
Reach me down the raisins in that cupboard
by you, that's a dear."

Sally's ill-humor curled up at the edges and
blew away as, all over again, she began to
be tickled by Flop's mother. Mrs. Merriam
was so different from Mom.

She was a bustling little woman who always said whatever was on her mind at the
moment, no matter to whom she was talking.
Just as she'd told Sally over the phone all
about Flop's allowance problems, so she
would have detained a tramp at the back door
to explain what she thought of the newest
cake mix. And though she was always in a
hurry to get things done, she had to hurry

twice as fast to undo them when she found they'd been done wrong. She'd scold Flop one minute, and forget the next what Flop had done. Pretty as a plump little bird, with black hair and clear skin like Flop, she was so pleasant to look at that Sally never minded what she said.

Now she snatched the flour from Flop and the raisins from Sally, and began vigorously measuring and mixing. Flop lingered nearby, watching wistfully.

"Can I bake cookies?" she asked.

"My goodness, no!" cried Mrs. Merriam. "After that last time? No, that was the macaroni, spilled all over the silverware drawer — and who's to clean it out? *You* were supposed to do that, miss!"

Flop backed hastily toward the door, signaling Sally to come along. "I promised to show Sally the dress you made."

"Oh, my, yes! Sally, you tell your mother she's welcome to the pattern any time." Mrs. Merriam beamed, promptly forgetting the spilled macaroni. "I know it would look lovely on you."

"I don't think Mom would have time to make me a dress," Sally interrupted. It wasn't polite to interrupt, but with Mrs. Merriam there was nothing else to do. "She's awfully busy at the shop, and she doesn't like sewing very much anyway."

"Dear, dear, life is like that, isn't it?" Mrs. Merriam shook her head sadly, but Flop pulled Sally hastily away before her mother could expand on the idea.

Up in Flop's room, Sally admired the new dress, but agreed with Flop that it wouldn't be right for her at all. "I look awful in ruffly things," said Sally. "Or, anyway, I *feel* awful and that's the same thing. I wish I could wear shorts and tee shirts and sneakers all year round."

"Ugh, I'd hate it!" Flop shuddered. "I look like a horror in shorts anyway. My legs are too fat. And a stomach bulge looks twice as big in shorts." Flop looked at herself in the mirror and sighed. "I guess I'm just doomed."

"Your mother's plump, and she's cute as a doll," Sally reminded her. "And boys must like plump girls, because you practically never see a plump old maid. Old maids look more like Miss Dickerson." Sally wrinkled her nose.

"I guess that's right," Flop conceded, much cheered. She sat down at her dressing table and, opening one of the many little jars that littered it, began to cream her face.

Sally picked up one and then another of the jars and bottles to study their labels. "You've got lots of new ones. Have you been sending for samples again?"

"Dozens of them," said Flop. "I don't know what some are supposed to do, but I'm trying them all anyway. The older a girl gets, the more care she has to take of her skin, you know."

Sally started to laugh, but the sound came out more of a sigh. Flop sounded so grown-up when she talked of beauty care and boys and parties; sometimes she made Sally feel very young and not too smart. And there was the way she felt about Jeff Donnelly, who'd never said more than hello to her in his life. Going past his house again and again, coaching other girls what to say about her when he was within hearing, treasuring that silly key ring he'd happened to drop one day — not even a key on it, just his identification tag.

Flop had looped a blue satin ribbon through it and hung it beside her mirror. Sally poked it with one finger. "Still haven't given it back to him, have you?"

"Of course not. I shall keep it *forever*."

"I don't know why. If you gave it back, he'd at least have to talk to you."

"Not yet." Flop looked mysterious. "All he'd say now is 'thanks.' But someday, when he knows me better, it will be a conversation piece; he'll just die of curiosity, trying to find out where I got it, and when, and why I kept it."

Sally sighed a little more audibly. Floppy sounded as if she were peering through a telescope at a foreign land that she couldn't wait to reach; and Sally was quite happy where she was.

She studied her own face in Flop's mirror. Her golden-brown eyebrows and lashes were pale in contrast to her deeply tanned skin. She decided she looked like the negative of a picture — all the light places dark, and the dark ones light. Her hair was pulled back so tightly that her eyes tipped up a bit at the corners. Her arms, shooting out of the skimpy tee shirt, were browner even than her face, and hard from hours of tennis. Sally had to smile at the picture she made in Flop's mirror; she so plainly didn't belong in this ruffly pink room.

"I look more like a boy," she said aloud.

Flop said consideringly, "You wouldn't if you quit yanking your hair back so tight. You ought to have a permanent and let it hang loose around your face. Maybe catch it back here — with a little blue bow barette to match your eyes. . . ."

Sally laughed. Color washed her brown cheeks. "Wouldn't that be something, though? Me in a bow!"

"Well, *I* think you'd look pretty."

"I don't want my hair hanging on my neck; it'd feel too hot when I play tennis." Sally dismissed the idea. "I'd better be going home, Flop. Mom said to put the potatoes on."

Flop followed her to the door. As Sally swung onto her bicycle, Flop called after her, "Well, don't bother anymore about what Miss Dickerson said. It isn't true, not a word of it."

A little glow warmed and spread inside Sally's heart. "I guess nobody ever had a better friend than Flop," she thought contentedly.

Sally decided to make some cookies after she'd put the potatoes on to boil. Mom wouldn't mind, and Flop loved cookies, the richer the better.

"I'll make the kind with dates and nuts," she planned, "sprinkled with powdered sugar and little cinnamon candies." In her enthusiasm over the project, Sally almost forgot entirely her earlier worries about business at the shop.

11 ⸻

BUT WHEN MRS. BARRETT came home, all Sally's anxiety came racing back. Mom looked tired as she tied on her apron and started snipping up vegetables for a salad.

Sally gave her a hug. "The potatoes are almost done, Mom. And I baked cookies. And, Mom, I darned four pair of my socks."

"Well, what a good helper!" Mrs. Barrett smiled. But the smile faded as she turned to the refrigerator, and suddenly Sally couldn't stand the weight of her worries any more.

"Mom," she burst out. "Is something wrong at the shop?"

Mrs. Barrett gave her a startled look. "Wrong? Why, what gave you that idea, Sally?"

Sally already regretted asking, but — no, she *wasn't* sorry. She just had to know.

"Are we awfully short of money? Isn't business good, or something? You've been at the shop so much, and — sometimes you and Dad talk . . ."

Sally's voice trailed off. She felt very foolish when she saw the tiredness on Mom's face vanish into familiar laugh lines. "Well, I just wondered," Sally finished lamely.

Mrs. Barrett sat down on the kitchen stool. "Now that you've brought it up, I might as well tell you," she said. "We were going to talk to you and Dennis soon, anyway, because we do need your help in what we're planning. No, business isn't bad; it's very good. And that's the problem. Your dad hasn't nearly room enough at the shop; he ought to build a much bigger place, and take on one or two more men. If he did, he'd be better off in the long run, I'm sure."

"Then why doesn't he go ahead and do it?" asked Sally. "*I* would."

Her mother laughed. "Well, that's what I'd do, too — rush right in and start building without giving it a second thought. But your dad's more practical; he has to figure all the angles first. So I've been adding up exactly how much business we've done each month this year, and figuring how much more we could have handled if we'd had the space and what the profit on it would have been."

Sally shook her head. "I guess you made straight A's in math."

"I never got more than a C," her mother said ruefully. "But I worked so hard to get even that, I guess it stayed in my head. . . . Well, time to start the pork chops."

Sally got out a skillet and set it on the stove. "Is Dad going to build, then?"

"I think so. The men at the bank told him he'd be foolish not to. They offered to lend him the extra money he'll need, but you know your dad—he's death on borrowing. He's been trying to figure every possible way to raise enough without that — or at least without having to borrow very much."

"Can he do it?"

"He can if we all help. And I told him we would. I promised we wouldn't spend a single extra penny till he had the new building up and the loan paid off. We'll skip our vacation at the lakes——"

"Oh, Mom!"

"I know. But renting a cottage for two weeks and making the trip costs a great deal, you know. We'll save almost two hundred dollars by staying home."

"Well, I guess I don't care *too* much," Sally said, with almost convincing cheerfulness.

"My tennis will be a lot better for not missing so much practice."

Her mother's warm smile acknowledged her effort. "We'll still have our two weeks at Grandma's in August, when we help her with her canning. You always have fun there."

Sally sighed. "I wish I could get a job. Denny's looking for one right now."

"He is? Well, bless his heart! I didn't think he'd ever take that much time from tennis."

"I could get lots more baby-sitting if I could just stay out later, Mom. Practically *nobody* wants a baby-sitter who has to be home by ten o'clock."

"I know, Sally, but at thirteen a full night's sleep is more important than money."

"Every now and then wouldn't hurt," Sally coaxed.

Mom didn't answer, so Sally dropped the subject. If it were just her mother she had to persuade, maybe the rule might be relaxed a bit, but Dad was a different story. Oh, dear, what could she do when her father was *so* old-fashioned . . . and so strong-minded when it came to saying "No"?

The next day was June at its best, dry and sunny and just cool enough after the rain to be ideal for tennis. Sally hurried through her household chores to clear the way for practice.

Mrs. Barrett had decided to wash. Sally, carrying out baskets of clothes to hang on the lines, remembered that this was the year Mom had planned to get a dryer. That was one of the things that would be postponed now, but Sally knew her mother would never mention it, not even by a single sigh on washday to indicate how much harder the work was without it.

"She's an awfully good sport," Sally thought with pride. Secretly she promised herself to do as well. No complaints, not a one. And no wheedling to get a penny extra when her allowance ran short.

Sally's spirits billowed like the sheets in the breeze, now that her weight of worry about the shop was lifted. Cutting expenses to get ahead wasn't anywhere near as bad as cutting expenses because there just wasn't any money.

Dennis was mowing the lawn. As he ducked under the washlines, Sally said, "What luck did you have yesterday, Denny?"

"One store said they'd put me on as delivery boy next time they had an opening. And I filled out an application at Western

Union for messenger. I'm going to try some more places today."

"Did Dad tell you why we have to be careful about spending?"

Dennis nodded. "I'm all for it."

"So am I. But I wish I could make enough somewhere for tennis balls. It's awfully hard to buy any out of my allowance."

"My racket's what's going to give me trouble." Dennis frowned. "It won't take another restringing; the frame's cracked. I'd sure like to get a new one before the tournament."

"Can't you charge it at Leed's? And pay a little something every week out of your allowance?"

"I'd be paying till Christmas. Gosh, a good racket costs at least twenty or thirty dollars!"

"Ouch!" said Sally respectfully. "Mine better not wear out — not ever."

"What you're going to need is strings," Dennis warned her. "How long you been playing on that set anyway? Ever since you got the racket? That was for your birthday two years ago, wasn't it? No wonder they're gone."

"They *are* kind of frayed, but I guess

they'll last," Sally said doubtfully. "Does stringing cost a lot, Denny?"

"Ten or fifteen dollars, at least. You couldn't get anything much better than grocery twine for less than that."

Sally winced. "Ten or fifteen dollars! Good grief, if a string breaks, I'll have to patch the hole with Band-Aids!"

"It isn't just the hole," Dennis reminded her, frowning at her ignorance. "It's the tension. If a string breaks, *all* the strings loosen up, and you might as well be hitting the ball with a" — he ducked as the breeze flapped the laundry in his face — "with a wet sheet."

Mrs. Barrett called, "Sally! Here's another load ready."

She was cleaning out the laundry tubs when Sally went down to the basement. "It's nice to have the washing caught up again," she said. "And it's drying so fast I believe I can start the ironing this afternoon."

"Oh, Mom!" cried Sally, round-eyed with horror at the prospect.

"Not you." Mrs. Barrett laughed. "You're done when you hang up that last load. I'll save your share of the ironing till tomorrow morning."

Sally said in relief, "I'm going to play tennis all afternoon. I can't afford to miss a single day's practice."

"Well, come on along, I'll help you get these out." Mrs. Barrett took one handle of the basket. "Up we go!"

"Mom," said Sally dreamily, as they worked side by side, pinning socks and jeans to the line, "did you ever win something? You know, like a trophy?"

"Well, let's see," Mom said very gravely, but with a twinkle, "I won a pin in Sunday school once."

"Oh, you know that isn't what I mean! I mean something *important!*"

"That pin was awfully important to me." Mom shook her head ruefully at the memory. "My oldest sister had won one like it years before. She kept it in a box in her dresser, and sometimes I borrowed it when she wasn't there; I liked to pretend it was mine. One day I broke the catch — wouldn't you know it? — and after that I was scared blue every time she went to her room, thinking she might decide just that moment to wear it. I tell you, I practically didn't eat or sleep for weeks; I was too busy studying my Sunday-school lessons so I could win a pin of my own. Your grandma was so worried about me. I got hollow-eyed and thin-cheeked and

went tiptoeing around, muttering to myself!"
Mom had to laugh again. She laughed till
tears stood in her eyes. "First thing after
I won my pin, I gave it to my sister and told
her what had happened to hers. And do you
know what she said? 'Oh, is that old thing
still around? I thought I'd lost it ages ago.'"
Mom wiped her eyes. "Kids!" she said. "They
suffer so much because they won't tell anybody what's the matter."

"Like me," thought Sally, "when I was
worried about our not having any money. I
could have asked sooner; maybe I was scared
to find out."

Dennis finished the lawn. "Hurry up," he
yelled at Sally, "we can get in some practice
before lunch."

The phone rang as Sally was pulling on
her tennis shoes. "Mom," Sally said anxiously, "if that's Flop, would you please tell
her I've gone and you don't know where?
If she knows I'm at the courts, she'll go there,
too, and Mr. Cochran doesn't want me to
play tennis with her; he says it'll spoil my
game."

Mrs. Barrett, with her hand on the receiver, said slowly, "Are you being honest
with her, Sally, by avoiding her instead of
telling her straight out?"

"I *can't* hurt her feelings, Mom! She's my best friend!"

"That's what I meant," said Mom. She silenced the jangling phone by lifting the receiver, and Sally, to her relief, heard her talking to Dad about coming down to sign the papers required by the bank.

But as Sally rode beside Dennis to the courts, she puzzled over her mother's last remark. It just didn't make sense at all — "That's what I meant," when Sally had said Flop was her best friend.

Sally frowned and gave it up. She hated to think it, but sometimes Mom reminded her a tiny, tiny bit of Miss Dickerson.

12 ═══════

AS THE TOURNAMENT came closer, Sally's stomach was constantly fluttering with butterflies of distrust. She practiced every afternoon at the courts till it was too dark to see the ball. When she couldn't get Dennis or Mr. Cochran as an opponent, she pounded the bangboard till it quivered.

Nobody now had to remind Sally it was bedtime; she knew how important it was to her game to get her full quota of sleep. She gave up eating ice cream and candy and cookies between meals, even refused desserts.

"Cuts your wind," she explained to her mother. "Athletes have to watch their diet very carefully."

Dennis hooted, "Look who's an athlete now! Next thing, she'll be giving us that line about being a champion."

"Well——" began Sally hotly, and then

fell silent. Denny wouldn't trap her into any such claim again; he'd made far too much fun of her already. Mr. Cochran had promised he'd tell her when she was a champion. She'd just wait till *he* said it, and then even Denny would have to believe it.

Mr. Cochran had mailed in their entry fees to ensure that their names would be included in the draw.

"There'll be a lot more entries in this tournament," he explained. "They'll make up the draw sheets the night before and have them already posted when we get there."

For a moment the word didn't sink in; then Dennis and Sally both cried, "We! Are you going, Mr. Cochran?"

"Well, I should hope so. I have to see what kind of coach I am, don't I? I thought we'd drive over about ten o'clock; they won't get started much before that."

A great weight rolled off Sally's heart. She had dreaded asking Dad for bus fare, when everybody was so proud of the savings they were making. Now she wouldn't have to.

The exciting Saturday came at last. Sally squinted anxiously at the sky as she took her place in Mr. Cochran's old convertible.

"It's going to rain," she said. "Look at that cloud."

"You're crazy," Dennis scoffed, but Mr. Cochran eyed the cloud more respectfully.

"Might at that, but I'd say no more than a shower. It won't hurt the Maryville courts, the way it would ours. They're well-drained clay."

Sally took another look at the cloud and then sat on her racket. "Go ahead and laugh, Dennis Barrett," she retorted to his snickers. "Guess I know better than to let a good racket get rained on! Especially when it's my only one."

Within five minutes Dennis was sitting on his racket, too, for it did rain — briefly, but hard. Mr. Cochran got the top up, but only after a tussle with the mechanism that cost them minutes and left all three damp, draggled, and uncomfortable.

"Didn't you bring extra clothes?" Dennis frowned at Sally as he unpacked fresh shirt and shorts at the Maryville courts.

"These are my only ones." Sally smoothed her new tennis dress anxiously. "Do I look awfully wrinkled, Denny?"

"You sure aren't any glamour girl," Dennis admitted.

Sally felt damper and more uncomfortable than before. She edged over to look at the big white square of cardboard tacked to a post outside the courts. Her own name looked out at her with the startling importance of a newspaper headline. "Sally Barrett, Fairfield." Linked with it was another name, "Teresa Fox, Maryville."

Teresa Fox. That would be the girl Sally played first. The only girl she played, if she lost. Sally shivered. A tight discomfort took hold of the bottom of her stomach; her tennis racket felt huge and awkward in her hands, and her feet were leaden weights.

"I wish I hadn't come," she thought in sudden panic. "Oh, I wish I could go home right now!"

She whirled around and almost bumped into an older girl who had been reading the draw over Sally's shoulder.

"Whoa there, youngster," the girl laughed, catching her arm as she stumbled.

Sally hated being laughed at, and she despised being thought a youngster. She pulled back from the stranger's touch.

But the girl didn't seem to notice. "You're from out of town, aren't you?" she asked.

"Fairfield," said Sally shortly.

"Mmmm." The girl ran a quick eye over the draw. "That makes you Sally Barrett, doesn't it? I'm Jane Anderson."

It was Sally's turn to glance at the girls' draw. Yes, there was Jane Anderson's name.

At the very top. Sally knew what that meant. If your name headed the draw, you had been rated the best player — seeded number one. Mr. Cochran had explained how the tournament manager seeded the two or four best players, writing their names in at top, bottom and middle of the draw before drawing the other names at random out of a hat, so they wouldn't meet and beat each other in the early rounds.

"That way he's sure of providing good matches in the semis and finals," Mr. Cochran had said, "when the tournament gets its biggest audience. Otherwise the finals might be played between the champion and some very poor player who was just lucky in the draw."

So now, looking at the position of Jane's name on the sheet, Sally knew that she was rated the best girls' player there. Probably she had won the district tournament the year before.

"And I suppose she thinks she's got it all sewed up this year, too," Sally thought unreasonably. She looked at the tall girl beside her, and didn't like her one bit. Jane was too smiling, too sure of herself, too — too smooth, Sally decided unhappily, backing away to hide her own wrinkles.

Jane was again studying the draw. Now

she said, "Teresa Fox — she's your first match, isn't she? Well, she's a good little player, but just a youngster — like you."

Youngster, indeed — that settled it. Sally turned and ran. She ran until she dived headlong into Mr. Cochran's car.

"Sally! What on earth —— "

"I want to go home!" Sally cried. "I don't *want* to play in the tournament!"

Mr. Cochran said understandingly, "Sally, do you know what you've got? Buck fever. That means being scared silly. Everybody gets it their first tournament; some players never do quite lose it even after they know what it is and what to do about it. *I* didn't."

Sally looked at him unbelievingly. "*You* got scared?"

"Right down to my bones, Sally. My stomach tied itself into knots and my hands turned into feet. But there's a cure for it. You go right up to your opponent when your match is called and you say, 'This is my first real tournament and I'm scared to death.' Take my word for it — it works."

Out on the courts, men had been carefully chalking new lines where the rain had erased them. Now they finished, and the tournament manager began calling names from the list in his hand.

"Rolf Perkins and Sam Hayden! You boys both here? You can get started on the first court now." He called two more boys to the second court, and then a pair of girls to the third. Suddenly his voice jangled down every one of Sally's nerves.

"Sally Barrett and Teresa Fox!"

A small dark girl sitting on a bench behind the courts dropped her sweater and walked out onto the fourth court. Sally sat as still as if she were frozen to the car seat. Her mouth was so dry she couldn't swallow.

Mr. Cochran said gently, "Here you go, Sally — first step on the road to being a champion."

Champion.

Sally slid out of the car and stumbled toward the court. Her feet were numb. She was numb all over. Her eyes were big as saucers and they didn't see anything ... not until she reached the court, and there was the small dark girl holding out her hand.

Sally took it. Her voice was high and strange and parrotlike as she said, "This is my first real tournament and I'm scared to death. Isn't that silly?"

13 —————

MR. COCHRAN WAS quite right. The words
were magic. Even while the sound of them
still lingered in the air, Sally began to giggle.
It *was* silly to be scared of just a game.

"You're fooling me," Teresa said sternly.
"You're not scared at all. You only said that
to make me feel better, because I really am
scared." She stopped, and a startled look
crossed her face. "I mean, I really was."
Suddenly she giggled, too. "Why, Sally Barrett, it's going to be fun playing you!"

Sally realized in a very few strokes that
Teresa's game didn't match up to her own.
Teresa's strokes were nice; she used the
right ones in the right places, so she was being well taught. But her shots were still too
soft and uncertain to hold up against Sally.
Sally won in straight sets, 6–1, 6–2.

Imagine it — a victory already behind her!

The thought of it sent Sally bouncing off the court on a bed of clouds. She was still riding high when her second-round match was called. Another youngster faced her, and again Sally poured her best drives across the net to win.

"Look at that! I can take 'em!" Sally chanted. The clouds were a rosy mist all around her now.

Then abruptly Dennis thrust his racket through them, barring her way as she ran starry-eyed back to the car.

"Hi! I see you're still picking on kids in rompers," he teased.

His words punctured the clouds, and Sally was dropped with a jolt on the damp clay of the Maryville courts.

"Oh, be quiet!" she scolded her brother crossly. "I haven't seen *you* doing any giant-killing!"

"That's because you haven't been watching," Dennis retorted smugly.

Sally gave him a suspicious stare; somehow he was just too airily confident. What had happened? Very carelessly, as though she just happened to be passing that way, Sally sauntered past the draw sheets and took a quick look at the boys' draw.

There was Denny's name out in the third

round all right, and — Sally looked again —
why, he'd met and beaten the fellow whose
name headed the boys' draw! That meant
Denny had upset the number-one player!
Now he had a very good chance — almost a
sure chance — to win the cup!

"Oh, my!" Sally breathed. "Oh, my, I just
can't lose now!"

Her third-round opponent was another girl
no older than she. Behind her, Sally heard
Dennis murmur, "What luck! Every girl
tailored to your own size, straight out of
nursery school."

Sally was so indignant that her drives
fairly sizzled. She was still thinking up words
to squelch Dennis forever when she realized
that she had won again, and that this victory
put her into the finals — against a girl big
enough to impress even Denny. It was Jane
Anderson.

Sally's knees wobbled a little when she
walked out onto the court for this last battle.
It had been a long day and an exciting one.
Sally was tired. Her right arm had begun to
ache; her racket dragged on it heavily. Her
dress clung to her — damper now with perspiration than it had been with rain.

Jane squinted at the sky while Sally took
her place on the opposite baseline.

"Think the rain'll hold off?" Jane asked the referee.

Sally looked up at the cloud, too. There had been clouds all day long, but this one appeared to mean business.

"Better get started," the referee advised. "You girls don't need a warm-up, do you?"

His bright coin spun into the air; Sally won the toss. This gave her the choice of serving first or choosing the side on which to begin play. Sally elected to serve.

For a moment she toed the baseline, quelling the touch of panic that brushed down her spine. This match meant so terribly much to her; it could make her a champion.

"Service!" she sang out, and slashed a beautiful fuzzy new ball across the net.

Jane met it neatly. Her return dug into the damp clay at Sally's feet. Sally stepped back and swung. But the ball wasn't where it should have been; it had bounced straight up instead of toward her. Sally's racket caught it a moment too late and tipped it into the net.

Sally frowned. "Bad bounce," she thought. "I wish the court was dryer." Back at the baseline, she called again, "Service!"

This time Jane's return almost bounced backward toward the net, and Sally knew what she was up against. Not bad bounces, but chops — wicked, sharply undercut chops with a bounce made even lower by the damp surface of the court. Chops that could never be lifted back over the net by Sally's top-spin drive, her strongest, her winning stroke!

"Grief!" stormed Sally. She *hated* chops. Oh, yes, she knew the answer to them — more chops. But that meant long, slow, deliberate points — no flashing drives and dramatic rushes to the net — just endless chops, long ones and short ones, to the backhand and then to the forehand, exhaustingly patient.

At best, Sally's stock of patience was small. And now — tired from the long, exciting day, keyed up from too many hours of being constantly on the alert — she found herself with no patience at all. Fatigue frazzled the edges of her temper.

Defiantly she swung on Jane's next ball with a wild drive. Angrily she swung even harder at the next. Her returns went into the net, and the first game was over. One big important game lost, and in four straight points!

Hot tears stung Sally's eyelids; her temper crackled like the fuse of a firecracker.

"Hey!" Dennis murmured to her, as she

and Jane changed sides. "What's the matter, kid? Don't you know a chop when you see one?"

"Yes, I do!" Sally flared.

"Better start acting like it, then," he warned.

Sally's lower lip was thrust out obstinately. "I'll *make* her drive!" she whispered passionately. "Wait till my shots start clearing the net. They'll come so hard she *can't* chop 'em back!"

"I'm waiting," Dennis said briefly.

Again and again Sally's fierce drives went into the net. She was two games down. Three. Her tears were very close now — desperate and hot and angry.

And then the threatening cloud spilled over. Not seriously enough to stop the match, just a slow gray drizzle that soaked the already wet courts and clung damply to the balls, weighting them down like lead centers.

The spectators retreated to their cars. The referee tented a newspaper over his head. Sally fought doggedly on.

And suddenly one of Jane's wickedly undercut balls ticked the top of the net and fell sluggishly back on her own side! And then another. And another.

"It's the balls!" Sally almost cried the

words out loud. "They're getting too heavy to lift over the net with a chop. Now she'll *have* to drive!"

But Jane didn't. Over and over she struggled to lift those damp balls with an undercut shot. Sally overtook her lead and pulled ahead one game . . . two.

"The idiot!" Sally thought bewilderedly. "Why doesn't she give up her silly chop and drive?"

And then, with the set almost gone, Jane drove. A weak, high, looping ball that Sally pounced on like a tiger kitten. Jane's secret was out. She *had* no top-spin drive. She had perfected a beautiful, patient, almost errorless chop — and made it her whole game. When she couldn't use it, she was beaten.

But she'd been beaten by a rain cloud, not by Sally Barrett, and Sally knew it. Even the bravely shining cup presented to her at the conclusion of the match was no consolation to Sally on the long drive home. Mr. Cochran was deeply silent the entire endless twenty-five miles. Dennis, cradling his own cup, spoke only in occasional sputters.

"Driving a chopped ball!" he fumed. "Just plain flailing it!"

And a few miles later, "All you needed was a horse, and you'd have looked like that guy in the book — Don Quixote — fighting wind-mills!"

They were turning off the highway into Fairfield when Mr. Cochran spoke for the first time. "Why didn't you chop Jane's balls, Sally?" he asked. "Wasn't that what I taught you?"

Sally's cheeks burned bright red.

"I forgot," she said, very low. But she knew she hadn't forgotten; she'd been too angry and impatient to bother. She promised, "I'll remember it next time. Honest."

"Next time!" Dennis shrilled. "You think anybody would take you to State after the show you put on today?"

"State? The state tennis tournament at Kirkland? The big one?" Sally's eyes and mouth opened wide. "Dennis, are you going to the state tournament?"

14 ═══

STATE TOURNAMENTS WERE — well, they were
for big-name players. The matches were
written up on the sports page of the daily
newspaper; Sally always read every word
about them. Why, people even paid money to
see the finals, and the winner was invited
to compete in even bigger tournaments —
the sectional, even the national! Surely the
state tournament, played at a big private
country club in Kirkland, was far outside the
dream-boundaries of Sally and Dennis Barrett!

But here was Denny saying soberly, "Well,
I sure *am* going — if I can raise the money,
and I think I can. I've got a job halfway
promised. Doesn't pay a lot, but I've got till
August to save what I need."

"A job? Oh, Denny, you never said a word
about it!"

"I didn't know about it myself till today." Dennis grinned at Mr. Cochran, who smiled in return.

"If it's all right with my partner, Dennis is going to work for our construction company as water boy," Mr. Cochran explained. "We have the contract for the new high school, so we'll have a crew working right here in Fairfield all summer."

Sally said wistfully, "Don't they ever have water girls on construction jobs?"

"I'm afraid not," Mr. Cochran said regretfully. "But if I hear of anyone needing a baby-sitter, I'll recommend you."

"Be sure to tell them I have to be home by ten," Sally reminded him glumly. "They'll really be beating down the door for me."

Dennis put in, "Don't know why you want to go to Kirkland anyway. You'll just blow up like a skyrocket because you don't like the referee's haircut or something."

"No, I won't," Sally promised earnestly. "Honest, I won't, Denny."

"Hmph!" snorted Dennis.

Mom and Dad met them at the door, and exclaimed at sight of the two cups. "Wonderful! You *both* won? Tell us all about it, right from the start!"

Dennis, pleased and embarrassed, said,

"Aw, it wasn't much," and had to have the details of his matches pried out of him, question by question.

And Sally, who ordinarily would have rushed into a minute-by-minute description of the entire day, was equally reluctant to talk.

"What's the matter with you two?" Mom cried. "I thought you'd be screaming and waving banners if you won a big tournament like that!"

"Oh, it's not so big," Dennis mumbled. "Not compared to the state meet."

"So that's what's next." Dad nodded understandingly. "There's always a bigger giant to kill when you're really serious about a game."

Mom was frowning slightly, and Sally knew what she was thinking — how much would the state tournament cost?

"We're both going to earn our way to State," she said quickly. "Denny's almost got a job already, and I'm going to get one, too."

"Doing what?" Mom asked practically.

"Well, *something*," said Sally. "If I have to, I'll go door to door and ask to — to wash windows or shine shoes!"

Mom reached over and squeezed her hand. "Sometimes you do sound like a champion, Sally."

Sally was pleased at the compliment, though she didn't understand it. Being a champion meant winning something big and important, didn't it? Then how could a person *sound* like a champion?

That evening Sally and Dennis figured as closely as they could what the tournament would cost them.

"Remember it lasts a whole week, not just a day like this one at Maryville. Of course, *we* won't last a week, and we'll go home as soon as we get beat. But they'll probably only play one round of matches a day, so we should figure on a couple of days, even three."

"There's bus fare," Sally said anxiously.

"I called the bus station," said Denny, beginning a penciled column of figures. "Twelve dollars."

"Apiece?" gulped Sally.

"Yep. And, say, two nights at the Y. That's maybe another ten dollars apiece. And meals — I'm going to figure five dollars a day for me, that's thirty-two dollars. Entry fees —— "

"My head aches," mourned Sally.

"Five dollars an event. If I can get a partner, I want to enter doubles, too."

"I'll stick to singles," Sally said with a big sigh. "Don't think of any more things, Denny. How much does that add up to?"

"Forty-two dollars, so far."

"So far!" Sally cried in despair.

"And there will probably be things we forget, so we'll have to allow for them. One thing sure, I've *got* to get a new racket, and you sure ought to have a restring job. . . ."

"Hah!" said Sally. She left Dennis to his figuring and went away to do some of her own.

Baby-sitting would never earn her enough. What else could she do? Last summer she'd operated a cold-drink stand for almost a week — Floppy had helped; but they'd drunk most of the stock themselves, waiting for customers, and Flop had gained two pounds.

Housework? She couldn't ask Mom to make a job for her, not with everybody trying so hard to cut expenses. And other mothers would think her too young to be much help.

Errands, weeding gardens, mowing lawns — most families in Fairfield did that sort of work themselves, or had a regular boy or girl hired to do it.

Selling things door to door . . . Sally had sold Christmas cards last fall and made most of her Christmas money. She was a good salesman when it was something she believed in; the people she called on caught fire from her own enthusiasm. But what could she sell at this season that people really wanted? Absolutely nothing. Stationery, magazine subscriptions, general greeting cards . . . but people only bought those things when they wanted to be kind.

Sally fell asleep, still racking her brains for ideas — and woke the next morning to the biggest and best idea yet.

She'd start a nursery school!

15 ———

FIRST THING AFTER breakfast, Sally and Flop
made a list of every mother of small children
they knew. Then Flop went home to phone
her portion of the names, and Sally started
on hers.

"Mrs. Adkins?" she asked in her most
businesslike voice. "This is Sally Barrett. I
wanted to tell you I'm going to be taking care
of children here at home every afternoon,
and I'd be awfully glad to keep little Karen
for you sometime. I'm asking fifty cents an
hour or just two dollars for the whole afternoon. Why, thanks, Mrs. Adkins, I hope you
will try me out."

When she'd finished with her list, Sally
started on the yard. There ought to be a
sandbox. She'd ask Dennis if she could buy
a quarter's worth of sand from the big pile
on the job where he was working.

And toys. Lots of toys. Sally rummaged through the Barrett attic and came out with enough old dolls, push toys, and stuffed animals to keep half a dozen children busy.

It was too bad the yard wasn't fenced. Maybe she could fence a tiny bit herself, just enough to keep the very youngest children from crawling away while she played games with the older ones. After all, she had to be prepared to take care of several different ages at a time.

With an armful of kindling, she staked out what amounted to an oversize play pen, looping bright Christmas cord from stick to stick to make a barrier that might fool toddlers into thinking themselves fenced in.

When her preparations were completed, she called Mom to see them.

"Why, that's fine! Shows good thinking," Mom praised. "But what's going to happen to your tennis practice if you're baby-sitting every afternoon?"

"Oh, surely they'll take their kids home by five or so, won't they? I'd still have time for a set before dark. And I can always practice against the house while I wait for customers."

Mom warned, "It won't be all fun, you know. It's harder to keep children amused all afternoon than to sit with them at night when they're asleep."

But nothing could dampen Sally's enthusiasm. "Just think of all the money I'll earn! I'll be *rich* by August."

So interested were Sally and Flop in planning games for their future customers that the afternoon flew by. Not till Dennis came home, tired, sunburned, proud of having put in his first day on the payroll, did Sally realize her own day had netted her nothing. For a moment panic nibbled at her. She had at the most six weeks to earn her tournament fund. If there were many days like this . . .

Nobody turned up the next day either. Nobody but Isabel Rooney, looking for a tennis match.

"I can't leave," Sally turned her down regretfully. "Somebody *might* come."

But it was a gorgeous day for tennis. Wistfully Sally watched Isabel pedal away toward the courts. This was the hardest part of the job, staying home when her whole heart was out on a sunny court.

By the third day even Flop was getting bored. "Why don't we skip a day and go swimming? It's so hot."

Sally shook her head. "Not me. I've just got to be here if someone comes, or they'd never try again."

"We-ell . . ." Floppy hesitated. "It's just that I've got a brand-new suit. . . . I bought it for camp, and I want to break it in a *little* bit. . . ."

"You go ahead," Sally insisted. "I can manage fine alone."

In mid-afternoon her patience was at last rewarded. A mother brought her little girl to stay while she shopped. Sally played dutifully with the docile three-year-old, collected her money at five thirty and felt like a banker.

She phoned Floppy immediately to tell her all about it, but found her friend strangely unimpressed. "I don't know if I can get over there tomorrow either," Floppy said vaguely. "I think maybe I'll go swimming again."

"Two days in a row?" cried Sally. This certainly wasn't like the Floppy she knew, who had to be badgered to exert herself. Sally said suspiciously, "How come you're so crazy about swimming all of a sudden?"

"Well, everybody says it's *wonderful* for your figure. You know that."

"Sure, I know it. I've been telling you that for ages, but you still didn't go." A sudden thought made her ask, "Who was there?"

"Who?" Floppy sounded even more vague. "Oh, lots of the kids . . ."

"Like Jeff Donnelly, maybe?"

"Let me think," Flop said with elaborate casualness. "Yes, he did come by for a while."

"I knew it," said Sally. She hung up in disgust. There went her nursery-school helper. If there was a chance of Jeff reappearing, Flop would spend every waking moment at the pool. What was so wonderful about boys? Sally puzzled anew, feeling somehow young and ignorant before Flop's greater worldliness.

The next afternoon brought new customers — twin boys, Bob and Bill Monroe. They were about five years old, and built like miniature prize fighters. When their mother left to go to her dentist date, the boys stared at Sally with identical black scowls and outthrust underlips.

"Well!" cried Sally cheerily. "What shall we play?"

"Don't want to play," said Bob. Or maybe it was Bill.

"How about trucks?" urged Sally. "Just wait till you see our beautiful fire truck. And there's a dump truck and —— "

While she talked, she steered the boys forcefully around the house, and now they spotted the play area in the back yard.

"Yow!" yelled Bill — or Bob — breaking away from her.

"Wow!" screamed Bob — or Bill — taking off after him.

They fell on the line-up of trucks with ear-splitting shrieks.

"Mine!"

"Mine!"

"You let go — I saw it first!"

"I did, I did!"

Sally separated them with difficulty. "Look, there's plenty for both of you. Let's make a town. . . . You be the fire chief over here, and you be the man who builds roads, and I'll run a grocery store. . . ."

Peace was restored. It lasted till Sally put in a call to the fire station — "Help, help, my store's on fire!" — and the twin with the dump truck knocked over the fire engine in his hurry to reach the store first.

Bob hit Bill in the stomach, and Bill kicked Bob. They both fell down, locked in each other's arms, and rolled screaming and biting across the yard, knocking over the playpen fence and crushing a flower bed.

When Sally finally separated them, Bob had a button off his shorts and Bill's tee shirt was torn. Both of them were muddy and grass-stained.

Sally was ready to cry. She took a twin

firmly by each hand, led them to the coil of hose, and washed them.

"Now you'll have to come in the house while I sew you up," she said, "instead of playing. So there. And it serves you right for getting mad."

"Who's mad?" asked Bill.

"Not me," said Bob.

"I guess her," decided Bill.

They followed Sally into the house, as mannerly as little cherubs, and stood stock-still, their noses puckering like rabbits', while she repaired their clothing.

"Something smells good," reported Bob.

"Cookies," suggested Bill.

"I want a cookie," said Bob.

Sally took them to the kitchen. Mom's eyes twinkled, but her face was grave as she handed out two cookies apiece.

"How's it going?" she murmured to Sally.

Sally rolled her eyes. "What *time* is it?" she whispered. "Is their mother getting a filling or a whole new set of teeth?"

"Three o'clock," Mom reported.

"You mean they've only been here an *hour*?" Sally staggered a little as she ushered her charges back to the yard. "There *must* be easier ways to make money," she thought; "I won't, I won't, I *won't* take care of children."

But when Mrs. Monroe at last appeared and counted out an impressive pile of change, Sally revised her opinion.

"I guess it couldn't *ever* be any worse than today," she decided. "So I won't quit now."

There was quite a steady trickle of youngsters all month at Sally's nursery school. One or two, usually; occasionally, none at all. After three straight afternoons of not seeing Jeff Donnelly at the pool, Flop lost interest in swimming and came back to help. But Sally couldn't count on her, for often Mrs. Merriam called her home to help get her clothes ready for camp.

"I wish I were going," Sally said. Camp was one of the extras the Barretts were giving up this summer.

"So do I. It'll be just plain stupid without you. I wanted to skip it, but Mother won't let me. You know what I bet? Miss Dickerson's been talking to her, that's what." Floppy's round face lengthened with gloom. "Mother's even made out a *diet* for me. Why, I'd *starve* if I didn't get something to eat over here."

Sally said uneasily, "I didn't know you were on a diet. Maybe you shouldn't eat stuff here."

"I thought you were my *friend*!" Flop cried.

"Well, I am —— "

"All right, then. Do go in and get us some cookies," Flop coaxed. "*I* don't dare; my mother might have talked to your mother about my diet."

Sally decided a few cookies more or less wouldn't make any difference. And, after all, she couldn't take sides against Floppy, could she? She waited till Mom was out of the kitchen, then helped herself to a double handful from the cookie jar. But she didn't enjoy her share, somehow. Maybe it was all right for Flop to fool *her* mother, but Sally had very few secrets from Mom.

16 ═══

TWO WEEKS BEFORE the state tournament Mrs.
Barrett had a long-distance call from her
mother.

"Can you folks come up a little earlier this
year?" Grandma asked. "It's been such a hot
summer, everything's ripening so fast I can't
keep up with the canning."

"Why, yes, it won't make any difference in
my plans," Mom said, considering. "Let's see,
if Mrs. Fuller's free to come take care of the
house for Dave and Dennis, I'll drive up with
Sally Monday morning."

Sally was jiggling up and down frantically
behind her.

"No, Mom, no!" she whispered loudly.

"Wait a minute, Mother, I can't hear,"
Mrs. Barrett said. "Sally, for goodness'
sakes!"

"I *can't* go, Mom! Not now. I'd get all out of practice before the tournament."

"Oh, the tournament — is it that soon? I didn't think about that." Mom picked up the receiver again. "I may be the only one coming this trip, Mother. Sally has a big tennis tournament coming up — the state meet in Kirkland — and she wants to keep in practice right up to the minute she leaves. . . . Yes, both of them are going; they're tennis mad this summer. . . . Oh, I know; I'm all for it myself. They'll learn a lot on a tennis court besides tennis. . . . Sally, your grandma wants to say hello and good luck, if she's not going to see you."

When the call ended, Mrs. Barrett said, "You won't have any vacation at all this summer, Sally. Not going to the lakes or camp, and now missing the trip to Grandma's."

"I know," said Sally, thinking of Grandma's cool, quiet house with the big rambling porches where she loved to lie and read by the hour, and the fascinating attic that she never tired of exploring, and the pleasant country roads where she could ride old Rusty. "But the tournament's all the vacation trip I want."

"I guess that's right," Mrs. Barrett admitted with a smile. "You don't think about much else nowadays but tennis. It's lucky the season's over by the time school starts, or you'd take two years to pass every grade." She picked up the phone book. "What's Mrs. Fuller's number, do you remember? I'd better call her right away to make sure she can come —— "

Inspiration hit Sally like a bursting rocket. "Mom! Why do we have to have Mrs. Fuller?"

"Why, to cook and clean and —— We *always* have Mrs. Fuller when we go to your grandmother's."

"Yes, but this is the first year *I'm* not going!" Sally cried excitedly. "And I can cook and clean! I do it all the time, helping you. Oh, Mom, can *I* have Mrs. Fuller's job?" Sally clasped her hands; her blue eyes were enormous with pleading. "Then I'd be *sure* to have plenty of money for the tournament!"

Mrs. Barrett said doubtfully, "But you've got your nursery school to keep you busy. You wouldn't have time."

"The kids are always gone by five, Mom. That's plenty early enough to start dinner."

"And the marketing — you'll have to plan your meals ahead and make out a grocery list so Dad could bring things home. . . ."

Sally's quick ear caught the change in tense. Her mother was actually considering her proposal. Sally hugged her in delight. "I know I can do it, Mom, I know I can!"

"I'd better have Mrs. Fuller do the washing and ironing, though; that would be simply too much for you. And the heavy cleaning." Mrs. Barrett tapped the phone book with her fingernail thoughtfully. "But I do believe you could manage the cooking . . . and it would be good experience. . . ."

Sally swung her mother in a joyous circle. The phone book went flying, and so did one of Mrs Barrett's braids. "Oh, swell, Mom! Thanks!"

"Better hold up on the thanks." Mrs. Barrett laughed a little breathlessly, freeing herself at last and pinning up the dangling braid. "You may not be so happy about your job after you actually get started."

"Oh, yes, I will, Mom; I *love* to cook. And think of the money I'll be earning. . . . How much money?" she suddenly remembered to ask.

"I'll talk it over with your dad. We'll see."

That evening, after a conference with Sally's father, it was decided that Sally should receive ten dollars a week for preparing the meals and keeping the house straightened up. Mrs. Fuller would do the rest of the work.

Ten dollars a week! That meant twenty dollars more for her tournament fund.

"I've got it made!" Sally figured exultantly. "With what I already have, and what the nursery school will earn in the next two weeks, I'll have enough for the tournament and extra clothes and everything!" For Sally had learned her lesson at Maryville; she wasn't going to get caught at another tournament with only one tennis dress to wear.

Before she left, Mrs. Barrett helped Sally plan the first week's menus. They included simple, familiar recipes, all of which Sally had helped prepare before, and many foolproof dishes that could be made quickly from cans or a mix. With Mom supervising, Sally got the family's entire Sunday dinner herself: Swiss steak and onions, simmered for two hours, with potatoes and carrots added the last half-hour; a combination salad of lettuce and chopped celery, radishes, cucumber, and green pepper; and raspberry shortcake — the shortcake whipped up in minutes from a package of biscuit mix, and the raspberries picked from the Barrett's own bushes, washed and sugared earlier in the day to form their own mouth-watering syrup.

Dad said with great satisfaction, "Well, if this is the way we're going to eat while you're gone, Mary, why don't you plan to stay all month?"

"Serve you right if I did just that," Mrs. Barrett said in mock indignation. "Then when Sally went to Kirkland, you could get your own meals."

"I forgot about Kirkland. Hurry back, Mary — please!"

"You make swell pancakes," Denny reminded him.

"I'm afraid I'd get pretty sick of pancakes three times a day. We'd better hope Sally doesn't quit on us before your mother gets back."

"And lose out on that twenty dollars?" Sally said blissfully. "Not a chance!"

Dennis said darkly, "Wait'll she gets mad at the stove for burning her finger or something. She'll quit fast enough then."

"I won't!"

"Now, Dennis ——"

"Housekeeping does take patience," Mrs. Barrett agreed. She looked at Sally with a little worried frown, and Sally, in panic, saw her chances for the job glimmering and fading.

"Honest, cross my heart, I won't get mad and quit," she promised fervently.

"It'd be the first time," Dennis mumbled.

Sally flung her heaviest artillery into the crumbling line of her defenses. "Look, if I don't do a good job — if I miss getting one single meal — I — I'll stay home from the tournament! Now do you believe me?"

17 ═══════

AFTER MR. BARRETT and Dennis left for work the next morning, Mrs. Barrett hurried around the house making final preparations for her trip.

She said to Sally, "Now listen, dear, we won't hold you to that promise you made last night. We know you'll do your very best, but if the job turns out to be just too much for you, ask Mrs. Fuller to take over."

"And let Denny crow about it the rest of his life? No, sir!" Sally declared. "Anyway, I won't have any trouble, Mom. Look how well the dinner turned out yesterday."

"But yesterday was a Sunday. You didn't have your nursery school to think about, too. If you find you can't manage the cooking with children here to take care of every afternoon ——"

"Oh, Mom, there's never more than one or two."

"Even so, they take time. And energy and patience. Well, give it a try and see how it goes. But don't be too proud to call for help if you need it. Let's see, what day do you leave for Kirkland?"

"Monday — wow, just two weeks from to-day!" Sally glowed at the prospect.

"Then I'll try to get back the day before. But if I don't make it in time to see you off, good luck, Sally. And don't forget what Mr. Cochran's always telling you — there's more to tennis than hitting the ball."

"Okay, Mom," Sally said a little doubt-fully. Hitting the ball seemed plenty to her. Hit it hard enough to the right places, and how could you lose? But she wouldn't bother her head about it now.

She waved till Mom's car was out of sight, then went happily in to survey her realm. Well, it was *almost* her realm. Mrs. Fuller, of course, was already busy in the basement, starting the washing, but the kitchen was Sally's very own.

Sally studied the day's menu, wishing it were much more complicated so she'd have an excuse to begin on it immediately. But there wasn't a single dinner item needing her attention till late afternoon, and lunch was only soup and sandwiches.

Sally went out to the back yard and straightened a few wobbly pickets in the playpen fence. She set out the toys and games and dolls, ready for her first customer.

Then, though Mom had left the house in apple-pie order, Sally dutifully made the rounds of the rooms, picking up yesterday's newspaper, making the beds, setting a chair or hassock more exactly in place.

"Ten dollars a week for doing *this?*" she marveled. "What a setup!"

She helped Mrs. Fuller hang out the clothes, and told her all about the coming tournament. Mrs. Fuller listened amiably, but her knowledge of tennis was very scant.

"It beats me, anybody wanting to run around like that in this hot sun," she said, shaking her gray head. "I'd be afraid of heat prostration myself. Now, when I was a girl, I played croquet myself. That's much more suitable for a young lady, it seems to me. And it takes skill, don't you think it doesn't! If I do say so myself, I had quite an eye for the wickets. . . ."

Before Mrs. Fuller finished her reminiscences, the morning was gone, and Sally was thoroughly sorry she'd ever mentioned sports.

But when the last sock was on the line and Mrs. Fuller had gone home, the house seemed so still and lonely that Sally would almost have welcomed another blow-by-blow description of a croquet match. She wandered around the empty rooms. What a shame that Flop had to be at camp the same time that Mom was gone! She didn't even have anyone to phone.

Lunch hour made a cheerful break, but it was over too soon, and Sally was alone again.

No mother appeared with a child for Sally to tend. That wasn't unusual; Monday was always a poor day for Sally's nursery school.

Restlessly Sally took racket and ball to the side yard and practiced a brisk half hour against her wall. Then she wandered back into the house, got out the Mason jar that held her tournament fund, and counted and recounted the nickels, dimes, quarters, half-dollars, and dollars she'd hidden here. What a long, long time it took to save a lot of money. The young Barretts had had one lucky break — Mr. Cochran had arranged a ride for them to Kirkland with a salesman friend of his who'd be going through town that day. So they had to provide bus fare for the return trip only. But even so, with entry fee and meals and lodging and the new tennis dress she simply had to buy, it was still going to be a pretty expensive weekend.

Sally kept her Mason jar hidden, for Dennis was beginning to ask her more and more suspiciously how her tournament fund was coming along. She knew he wouldn't let her go with him if there was danger of her running short and getting stranded in Kirkland with no money. Dennis, who had bought himself an expensive new racket with the very finest string job a neighboring city could provide, would have barely enough put away to cover his own needs.

"But with this housekeeping job, I don't have a thing to worry about now," Sally thought contentedly. "And the nursery school will keep on bringing in a little, right up to the Saturday before we go."

She went out again to survey her kitchen proudly. It looked almost like an especially tidy battleground in a child's playroom, with the pots and pans and skillets and measuring cups already set up, like lines of soldiers alert and ready for the order to attack.

Sally moved them around into an even more efficient position, where they would be right at hand in the exact order she needed them.

"I don't see why it would hurt to start

things a *little* early," she sighed, unable to wait any longer to test her skill. "After all, when Dad's late, Mom keeps things hot for an hour or more and they still taste good." She squared her shoulders like a general about to march out before his troops and take personal command. "I think I'll begin right now!"

18 ─────

MACARONI. Well, that was simple enough.

Sally set water to boil, cooked a cup of macaroni in it till it was tender, and then combined it in a casserole with a cupful of coarsely grated cheese and a can of cream soup. On top she spread cracker crumbs and dots of butter, then set it in the oven. In less than half an hour it would be bubbly hot, with a crisp brown crust.

With her macaroni and cheese Sally planned to serve hamburgers. She had already mixed the ground beef with cornflakes, egg, and seasonings; now she shaped the mixture into balls, arranged them in a baking dish, and set it in the oven with the macaroni.

Sally consulted her menu. They were having peas, so there was nothing to do there but empty a can into a saucepan and set it on a top burner.

"But I might just as well do it now," Sally decided, "so I don't forget. I can keep the heat down low."

Salad. Mom had written "fruit salad"; that gave Sally's imagination a lot of leeway. Since time was what she had too much of, she planned a very elaborate salad, including many, many tiny melon balls, carved from a cantaloupe and a watermelon slice.

The day was hot, and the job slow and tedious. Sally took her materials out onto the cool front porch and set to work carefully. If a melon ball didn't come out perfectly round, Sally ate it. She had eaten quite a lot of them by the time she had a bowlful that satisfied her.

And time — that had been far too plentiful — had somehow vanished!

Sally looked up, startled, at the sound of Denny's bicycle tires in the gravel of the driveway.

"Is it that late *already?*" she cried.

"What's burning?" Denny sniffed and frowned.

"Grief!" screamed Sally, scattering melon rinds as she ran to the kitchen.

The smell was coming from the peas; they

had boiled dry and were burned to the pan, looking like nothing so much as a handful of hard brown BB's.

Another smell was coming from the oven. Sally yanked open the door and stared in dismay at her casserole and the hamburgers. They were meant to be brown, but not *that* brown!

"Aw, brother, and I'm *hungry!*" Dennis groaned. "What a life for a working man — starved to death in his own home!"

For once Sally had no retort to make. She stared at the ruins of her dinner while tears welled in her eyes. Why, the crust on the macaroni was so hard it would take a cleaver to cut it! She couldn't serve something like this for her first meal on her own; Dad would send for Mrs. Fuller before he took his second bite.

Sally made a lightning-quick decision.

"You go take your shower, Denny. I'll cook something else."

Dinner that night was a little late, but it satisfied even hungry Dennis. Tiny boiled new potatoes with cream sauce, green beans, pork chops, and the impressive melon-ball salad that had caused all Sally's troubles (well, not *all* her troubles; Sally was honest enough to admit that her impatience to begin was the main reason for the disaster). Except for the salad, the menu was exactly what Mom and Sally had planned for Tuesday night, so the ingredients were already on hand.

"And tomorrow night we'll just have what we were supposed to have tonight," Sally figured, "so I'll be even again."

Even, that is, except for money. For on Tuesday Sally took enough from the treasured hoard in her Mason jar to buy more ground beef and the other materials she needed to repeat Monday's menu. She couldn't ask Dad to buy them — not without confessing to her awful failure on the first try, about which Dennis (Sally remembered with gratitude) hadn't said a single word.

Sally's second try at the macaroni-and-hamburger dinner was so successful that even Dennis grudgingly admitted she was a pretty good cook — when she put her mind to it.

But, counting her tournament fund that night as she did every night, Sally thought in alarm that she'd *better* put her mind to it or this job would cost her more than she was being paid. It was frightening to see her fund shrink instead of mount up. And today again there had been no children at her nursery school.

"Well, I can still make it," Sally figured

determinedly, "*if* I don't have any more accidents in cooking, and *if* I have a good steady number at the nursery school all this week and next. It just can't go on like this. Somebody's *bound* to come tomorrow."

Wednesday Sally had eleven children on her hands!

19 ———

SALLY WAS PRACTICING at her bangboard wall when that awful afternoon began, and certainly the sight of a car stopping seemed anything but awful. She dropped her racket and ball and ran out to the curb.

It was Mrs. Adkins, bringing Karen. "I'll be gone most of the afternoon," she said. "Our service club is entertaining at the hotel. I wouldn't be surprised if it meant quite a lot of business for you today."

That sounded just fine to Sally. She took the little girl around to the sandbox, but before she could collect spoon and water and muffin tins to start her making sand pies, another car stopped. It was Mrs. Monroe's.

Sally looked at Bob and Bill doubtfully. "Say, I've got a great idea — I found our old boxing gloves the other day. I'll square you off a ring and you can really wear each other out."

She got the gloves, but before she could make a ring, another mother came.

"Grief, Mrs. Adkins was right," Sally thought distractedly, running around to the front of the house. "Every mother who ever left her children here must belong to that club."

She had just gathered in the new children when a wild shriek rang out in the back yard. Sally sprinted around the house. Bob and Bill had wriggled the boxing gloves on, but instead of battling each other, they had started on little Karen.

It took force to rescue Karen, but Sally had just accomplished it and restored peace when she heard still another car stop.

"Oh, no, not *another* kid!" Sally hoped fervently, trotting around to the front. It was a car full of them, including two babies.

Sally took a baby under each arm and herded the others toward the back yard. Noise greeted her as she rounded the house — noise that swelled into the familiar volume of Bob's and Bill's yells. They had tried to take a toy from the other children and met with a combined force bigger than theirs. Bill's nose was bleeding.

"Well!" exclaimed Sally, settling the babies in the playpen. "I guess everything's happened now."

It hadn't.

Bob and Bill tore up the playpen fence to get sticks for guns, and the two toddlers staggered happily away. Sally collected them and rebuilt the fence, but in the meantime Bob and Bill remembered the hose and where to turn on the water. Before Sally could wrestle it away from them, everybody, including herself, had been liberally squirted. It took an hour of the hardest romping Sally could invent to dry the children out.

By the end of that time Bob and Bill had disappeared.

Sally looked around for them in increasing alarm. She searched and called till her throat was hoarse and her heart pounded with fright.

Had they got out into the street? Could they have tumbled down the outdoor basement steps?

She loped up and down the block; she toured the alley; she scratched her legs clambering over the pile of fireplace logs beside the garage. She searched the house. And over and over she circled the yard, shouting, "Bob! Bill!"

Her frantic searching served one good purpose. It kept the other children intently interested and good as gold, as fascinated as if they were watching a television western.

Sally was passing the garage for perhaps the twelfth time when the faintest of giggles stopped her. She stared upward.

Bob and Bill were perched on the garage roof, their small heels braced against the eaves trough, their hands clapped over their mouths to silence their giggles.

"Oh!" stormed Sally, her relief giving way almost immediately to sizzling indignation. "Oh, you horrible little — you *brats*, you! Just you wait!"

She ran to the ladder leaning against the garage and mounted it with fire in her eyes. A car stopped at the front curb, then another and another. Sally didn't hear. It wouldn't have mattered if she had. Not at this point.

Down the ladder she lugged the struggling, kicking twins, and on the bottom step sat down and vigorously spanked them both. The twins screamed. The other children howled in sympathy.

"*Well!*"

At the explosive sound, Sally jumped. Bob and Bill promptly escaped. They ran to the indignant woman who had just appeared around the house, in the forefront of the entire group of mothers.

"Mommy! Mommy!" the twins yelped in chorus. "She hit me!"

Their faces were scarlet with anger and grimy with tearstains. The climb to the garage roof had left their hands and knees black. Bill's sunsuit was still smeared from his nosebleed earlier in the afternoon.

"Well!" their mother exclaimed again. "A *fine* place to leave innocent little children! If I'd dreamed how they were being treated!"

Sally couldn't say a word. Her throat was choked to bursting. In furious silence she watched Bob and Bill's mother whisk her roaring young ones out of the yard as if rescuing them from a stalking tiger. Wordlessly she saw the other mothers gather up their children and hurry away.

An impressive pile of money sat in Sally's lap, but there'd be no more. Sally knew it as clearly as if every mother had said it aloud. This was the end of her nursery school.

"Oh, *grief!*" Sally burst out.

She grabbed up her racket and ball from the grass where she'd dropped them so long ago, before calamity struck. Wildly she took a swing at the stretch of brick wall.

The ball went high. Sally squeaked in horror and squeezed her eyes tight shut. There was an endless splintering sound. Gingerly Sally opened one eye. The dining-room window lay in a hundred fragments.

And in the very center of her racket two strings had popped.

20 _____

SALLY WAS HUDDLED on the grass, weeping, when Dennis came home a little later.

"Hey, what gives?" he asked quickly. "Now what's up?"

"I'll have to buy a new window! And I haven't enough money to get the racket restrung!" Sally sobbed.

"Wait a minute," Dennis begged. "Close the floodgates, for Pete's sake!"

Sally mopped her dripping cheeks and held out her racket.

"Look," she said in a strangled voice. The frayed ends of the broken strings curled upward dismayingly. "And look!" She gestured toward the gaping window. "Even my nursery school's finished. I spanked those horrible little Monroe twins and their mother saw me. *All* the mothers saw me."

"Must have been quite an afternoon,"

Dennis decided. "I don't suppose you went and lost your temper, by any chance?"

"Dennis Barrett, *anybody* would have gotten mad!" Sally cried out indignantly. "A person couldn't have stood any more!"

Or could she? Of course she'd been scared and upset when she thought the twins were lost, and of course it had been maddening to know they'd been sitting up on that garage roof all the time, laughing at her. . . . Still, should she have spanked them, or let their mother do it when she told her how they'd acted? Sally hadn't actually been trying to correct them; she was just plain mad.

"Dennis," Sally said miserably, "what shall I do about the racket?"

Dennis looked worried. "I don't know. *All* the strings will loosen up if we don't get these ends tied right away. Tell you what — I'll put it in the vise down on Dad's workbench and see what I can do. You go measure that window and call the hardware store about putting in a new glass. You're sure lucky the window on this side is small."

Somehow Dennis managed to pull out the two broken strings and tie the ends firmly at the base of the racket frame. But it was a hard, sweating, straining job. It took him the whole evening, and he blistered his fingers so badly when a string slipped out of his grasp that his own temper shot up dangerously near the exploding point. Sally thanked him meekly and repentantly, and stayed out of sight as much as possible till his blisters healed.

It was a gloomy week.

At the end of it Mrs. Barrett phoned to say she'd be home the following Monday, but not before Dennis and Sally left for Kirkland.

"How is the cooking going, Sally?" she asked. "Everything all right?"

Sally gulped and said in a small voice, "I guess so. I never have any leftovers."

She didn't mention the number of times she had thrown away food that hadn't turned out too well, each time buying new ingredients with her own money to try again. Sally still liked to cook, but it was an art she now viewed with more respect. Being responsible for preparing an entire meal was a lot different from just helping Mom.

Mom said, "I'm proud of you, Sally. I'll admit now I was just a little doubtful you could handle this job, but you're really growing up fast. Don't forget to ask Dad for your twenty dollars."

"I won't," Sally promised fervently. Without it she'd be in real trouble.

Sally turned the phone over to her father,

glad that no more was said about money. It was her secret how much of the twenty dollars was needed to replace the money she'd borrowed from her tournament fund for groceries. Sally was afraid if her mother knew, she wouldn't trust Sally with the job another time.

"And next time I wouldn't make near so many mistakes," Sally defended herself, "so it would *really* be a good-paying job."

Her father, obviously reminded by Mrs. Barrett, counted out twenty dollars for Sally that same night.

"Just so I don't forget," he said. "Anyway, I suppose there'll be things you want to buy before you leave."

"Oh, thanks!" said Sally, delighted with the impressive stack of bills and coins.

Dennis frowned. "You should have waited till Monday morning. She'll go nuts with all that."

"Is that so, Dennis Barrett! I've had money around the house all month without wasting it."

"Yeh, where you been keeping it?" Dennis asked curiously. "How much *have* you got?"

"Wouldn't you like to know!"

"I sure would."

"Well, you aren't going to." Sally tossed

her head. "I guess I'm old enough to manage my own affairs."

"Hah!" said Dennis. He looked pointedly at the new dining-room window above the buffet, and Sally blushed and swung indignantly out of the room.

Dennis followed her into the hall. "How much did that window cost?" he asked. "You never said."

"Good grief, you're a busybody," Sally evaded him crossly. "I never heard so many questions — and all of them about my business."

"Well, it'll sure be *my* business if you get stuck down in Kirkland with no money for the Y or something. I don't give a hoot how much you've got stashed away, just so long as it's enough to get you there and back. Because *I* sure won't have any extra for you."

"Who asked you for any?" Sally said haughtily. "Certainly not me. I'll have all I need."

She wished that she felt as sure as she sounded.

21 ═══════

THE DAY BEFORE Sally left for the state tournament Flop arrived home from camp, and almost immediately appeared at the Barrett house.

"I'm absolutely *starved!*" she cried to Sally. "You wouldn't think a camp that charged as much as the Umpqua would *dare* be so stingy with their old food!" She lifted the covers of the cake pan and the cookie jar, stared in dismay at their emptiness, and peeked into the refrigerator.

"Well, thank goodness," she said in relief, bringing out the remains of last night's cottage pudding and lemon sauce. "I was beginning to think your kitchen was as bad as ours. If Mother *has* baked anything, she's got it under lock and key."

"You're looking great," said Sally. "I never saw you so tan."

Flop groaned. "No wonder! Those coun-
sellors were murder this year. Every time I
tried to sneak a little tiny nap in the shade,
they pounced on me like — like vultures on
a poor innocent chicken. 'Come on, Felicia,'"
she mimicked in a high gay chirp, " 'we're
just starting out on a jolly boat ride . . . and
guess who's going to get to row all the way
across the lake!'" Flop said suspiciously,
"Do you suppose that Mother talked to them,
too?"

She added cream to the lemon sauce on her
big square of cottage pudding and carried it
out to the porch. "Where's all our happy little
customers? Oh, that's right, it's Sunday."

"It wouldn't matter if it were a weekday,"
said Sally with a big sigh. "You still wouldn't
hear the prattle of little voices. The nursery
school folded kerwham."

"What happened? Did you have a terrible
time managing them alone?"

Sally said ruefully, "I managed 'em all
right. Just wait till I tell you how."

She plunged into a description of the fatal
Wednesday afternoon and her merry-go-
round with the Monroe twins. "Horrible, horrible little creatures," she finished.

"I'm *glad* you spanked them!" Floppy said
staunchly. "It's plain nobody else ever did, or

they wouldn't be such horrors. I don't care if it did make all the mothers mad. You did just right!"

Sally said doubtfully, "Do you really think so? I've kind of wondered about it ever since. I mean, I did lose my temper. . . ."

"Well, who wouldn't? I guess Saint Peter would have whaled 'em after that."

"I don't know. Afterward I tried to think what Mom would've done if she'd been here — and one thing's sure, she wouldn't have blown her top the way I did. She'd have been just as worried, and maybe just as mad, too, when she found them. I can almost see the way she'd have looked, with her eyes snapping and her mouth set tight — she's looked that way at me and Denny, times when we got her pretty aggravated. And maybe she'd have marched them over to a corner and sat them down and told them to stay there till their mother came — but she wouldn't have yelled or walloped them."

Floppy said, "Well, of *course* not! But she's a mother. They're different."

"How do they get different," Sally puzzled, "unless they start in practicing *before* they're mothers?"

"Honestly!" said Flop impatiently. "I believe you've gone absolutely nuts, all alone here. It's lucky I got home when I did. You sound as if you'd been practically *brooding* over one little spanking that those miserable kids certainly had coming."

She scraped the last crumb from her bowl and got up. "Say, that was pretty good. I think I'll have another helping. That is, if you weren't saving it for dinner or anything."

"No, go ahead," Sally said. She followed Flop into the kitchen. How good it was to have her friend back again! And how nice to have Flop scattering the long, sober thoughts that had occupied her mind far too much the past week. "I guess it's time you did get back," Sally said more cheerfully. "I'd even started wondering if Miss Dickerson wasn't right after all, about my leaving the *Widget*."

Flop turned around from the refrigerator and stared at her, shocked. "Sally Barrett, I don't believe it!"

"Well, I was. Oh, I don't *really* think she was right, saying all those things. Only" — the doubts came back to assail Sally again — "only when I think back over everything — the fuss about the *Widget*, and the trouble with Bob and Bill — I can see that I do get mad awfully quick, and then I always *do* something without waiting to simmer down.

I mean, even if I'd walked around the block before I said anything, maybe I wouldn't have quit the *Widget*."

"You're *sorry* you quit," Flop said unbelievingly. "You'd rather have stayed on in that miserably insulting little spot they put you in —— "

"Well . . . but maybe this year I'd have tried harder to do a good job, and then they'd have given me more to do."

"I never thought I'd see the day!" Floppy cried. "After you told them off like that, to *think* about crawling back! Haven't you any pride?"

"I guess so," said Sally unhappily. "But I'd rather be proud about something I knew was right."

Floppy frowned at her doubtfully. "You sound so different—not at all like when I left. I don't know what's got into you."

"Oh, well . . . I guess it was silly. I haven't had a thing to do for ten days but poke around the house all alone and think. Can you stay for dinner, Flop? I'm celebrating because it's the last one I have to cook. We're going to have fried chicken and little biscuits and peach cobbler —— "

"Mmmm, don't say another word! Wait till I phone Mother."

Listening to Flop's more and more fervent pleas over the phone, Sally knew what the answer was before Flop replaced the receiver. Flop came back to the kitchen, scowling mutinously.

"That old diet!" she muttered. "As if it would make any difference just one night! Especially when I practically haven't had a single decent meal in two weeks."

Sally tried to comfort her. "Yes, but look how much you want to lose weight, Floppy. You're always talking about it."

"Of course I do, only you know as well as I do that it's glands and I'll have to have thyroid pills or something before it'll go away. But the doctor's told Mother I should try diet and exercise; he thinks I *overeat* — did you ever hear anything so silly? And he's got Mother so sold on it she practically counts every mouthful I eat. It's awful. And I just love chicken and biscuits." Floppy looked so wistful that Sally felt sorry for her.

"I'll save you some," she offered quickly.

"Will you?" Floppy hugged her joyously. "Oh, I just knew you would! You're the *best* friend. I'll come back just as soon after dinner as I can get away." She sighed blissfully. "Can you save me some peach cobbler, too? I *never* get dessert anymore at home. Gee, Sally, what would I do without you?"

22 ═══════

BUT AFTER FLOP had gone home, those worrisome doubts that had been plaguing Sally all week rose again around her head like a swarm of buzzing mosquitoes.

Was she really being a good friend to Flop when she helped her get around the diet rules her mother had laid down? Flop wanted terribly to be slim and pretty, to lose the roll of baby fat around her waistline and the double chin that kept boys from noticing her clear skin and heart-shaped face. Of course Flop wanted it to happen overnight; it was her favorite dream that someday their family doctor would give her some kind of pills that would make the extra pounds just melt away.

But apparently the doctor had had different ideas, or he wouldn't have given Mrs. Merriam that diet for Flop to follow. After all, it was by his orders that Flop was launched on this new program of less food and more exercise. Flop would lose weight, all right — Sally could even see a little change from Flop's two weeks at camp — but it would take a lot longer than overnight.

And even longer if her best friend sneaked her cookies and desserts and rich, butter-fried foods between meals.

"Oh, dear," sighed Sally, "everything was so simple when I just did things instead of thinking about them."

It came from being alone too much, she decided. And planning so hard to make the cooking turn out right, and worrying so much about having enough tournament money saved up. The summer before, Sally never would have bothered her head about such problems.

Maybe it was all part of growing up. Sally — when she had to be home by ten o'clock at night, or study when she wanted to see a movie — often thought longingly of how fine it would be to be grown-up. But perhaps, as Mr. Cochran told her so often about tennis, there was more to it than she suspected. Instead of being all fun and good times and freedom to do what she wanted, it was also developing a conscience and feeling responsible about things that she wouldn't have given a second thought to before.

Sally was unusually quiet throughout dinner and ate very little of her triumphantly successful final meal. Even Dad's high praise didn't lift her spirits, nor the sight of Dennis taking second and third helpings of practically everything.

"You've turned into quite a cook," Dad said warmly. "You mother couldn't have fed us one bit better than you have these last two weeks."

She could have done it easier, Sally thought, remembering the number of dishes she'd prepared twice to make sure they were up to her mother's standard. But that was a secret she'd never tell — anyway, not for years and years; maybe someday she'd tell her mother and they'd laugh about the time she'd had, but right now there wasn't anything funny about it.

Nor was there anything funny about waiting for Flop to reappear, now that Sally had made up her mind about what she had to do.

For once Sally hoped Mrs. Merriam would insist on Flop's staying home. But no; before Sally had finished the dishes, she heard Flop come running around the house to the back door.

"Hi, I saw the light in the kitchen, so I knew you'd be here. Oh, doesn't this kitchen smell *wonderful!* Do you know what *I* had for dinner — and on my first night home, when you'd think they could have rolled out the red carpet just once? One broiled hamburger — this big — and green salad and *spinach!* And only one glass of milk, and a slice of bread with so little butter on it I practically choked. I suppose they thought I'd put up a big fuss for more, but I didn't say one word, not one word. If that's the way they want to treat their only daughter — just starving her — okay for them."

While she talked, Flop lifted the cover from the empty skillet on the stove, looked into the pans, then peered in the oven.

"Where are you hiding the chicken and biscuits you saved for me?" she asked, puzzled.

"I didn't save any," Sally said, very low.

"You *didn't!* But you said . . . Do you mean your father and Denny ate *that* much? But how about the peach cobbler? You always have dessert left over." Flop turned toward the refrigerator, but Sally was standing in front of it.

"Flop, I've got to tell you something," Sally said, speaking very quickly before she

143

lost her courage. "I don't think I should give you food here that you're not supposed to eat."

"Mother phoned you — or phoned your dad," Flop guessed instantly. "But that's all right. She won't know."

"No, she didn't call," Sally said. "I decided it myself."

Flop stared at her, scandalized as if she'd caught Sally stealing eggs from a bird's nest or tormenting a dog. "But I thought you were my *friend!*"

"I am. That's why I can't do it. It isn't being a good friend to help you do things that hurt you." Under Floppy's round-eyed, totally disbelieving gaze, Sally's courage crumbled. She plunged on desperately.

"It's like your telling me I was right to get mad and spank the Monroe twins — or quit the *Widget* — when it wasn't right at all. Or telling me how great I'm doing in tennis when I'm just showing off instead of practicing the way I'm supposed to. I know it made me feel good, but — but a very best friend, like you are to me, should be honest, it seems. So honest that maybe it hurts. Because who else can you depend on?"

Why didn't Floppy say something? Sally would far rather have had her scream and yell or even throw things than just stand there silent, looking as if Sally had left her tied to a railroad track with the train coming.

"Please, Floppy," Sally said miserably, "don't be mad. I wouldn't have said anything if I didn't love you so much. But I *want* you to be the prettiest girl in high school — I *want* that stupid Jeff Donnelly to notice you and think you're wonderful — if that's what *you* want. And that's the way it'll be if you keep on this diet the doctor gave you. It isn't fair to help you cheat on it, and to keep pretending it's just glands and you'll outgrow it, when I know you really do eat quite a lot between meals —— "

"Well!" The word exploded from Floppy like a firecracker. "I'm very, very glad to know what you really think of me! Why don't you just call me an old fat hog and be done with it?"

"You aren't! I didn't say any such thing. It's just that you don't do a lot of running around to burn it up —— "

"Go ahead and say it! Now I'm lazy, too. A big fat lazy hog. Well, it's nice to know what your friends think of you!" Floppy's voice was high and shrill with fury and offended pride.

Sally began to cry. "You won't even try to understand —— "

"I understand, all right. I certainly do understand." Floppy's lips began to tremble. She winked her eyes very fast to hold back tears. "And don't think I'll put you to the trouble of spelling it all out for me again."

She whirled around and plunged toward the back door, but her tears had spilled over and blinded her and for a moment she couldn't find the doorknob.

Sally ran across the room and put a timid hand on her arm. "I'm sorry, Flop — *please* don't go! Oh, I wish I hadn't said a word — I don't care *how* much you get to eat over at our house. Please, Floppy!"

But Flop had got the door open and gone racing out into the summer twilight.

Sally turned back to see Dennis in the kitchen doorway. "What's all the ruckus?" he asked wonderingly. "I could hear you two yelling clear out to the street."

Sally brushed the tears from her cheeks. "Nothing," she mumbled.

"Well, it was the loudest piece of nothing anybody on this block ever heard." He waited, and then, seeing that his curiosity was going to go unsatisfied, he said cheerfully, "Oh, well, whatever it was, it'll probably blow over before you get back from Kirkland. Hey, you know how many hours till we start? Twelve. Just exactly twelve. How about that?"

23 ═══════

TWELVE HOURS UNTIL practically the biggest day in her life. Sally waited for excitement to take hold of the bottom of her stomach and creep up to her heart, erasing her misery over the quarrel with Flop.

But nothing happened. She just felt numb.

"I guess I'd better pack," she said, "so I'll be sure not to forget anything."

"Yeah, especially money," Dennis called after her as she started up the stairs. "How much did you say it was?"

But even this didn't strike a spark from Sally. She went on up to her room without answering.

There wasn't much to pack. Yesterday she'd washed and ironed her one tennis dress, but she'd have to wear that tomorrow, since they'd go straight to the club. The state tournament would have been under way several hours by the time the Barretts arrived.

Again Sally thought with regret of the extra tennis dress she'd planned to buy.

"But I don't suppose it'll make any difference, really," she thought. "In a tournament this size, with all those good players, I'll probably get beaten the very first round."

Mr. Cochran had warned them this might happen, and cautioned them not to feel too bad if it did. Sally and Dennis would be strangers to the tournament committee, with no record of important wins behind them to earn them a special place in the draw. So they might very well meet a champion their first match.

"If you do, don't let it scare you," he'd said. "Your games are good enough so that even a champion will respect you. Just play your very best, and I'll be proud of you, whatever the score. Remember, you're down there to watch and learn as well as play."

Sally finished her packing and stood at the open window that looked out toward Flop's house, down the block. The darkness outside was no blacker than her spirits.

"I ought to go to bed," she said at last, "and get lots of sleep so I'll be fresh tomorrow."

But tomorrow somehow didn't seem important anymore. Sally shut her eyes and tried to picture sunny courts and flashing white figures, but all she could see was Flop's hurt face, with tears blurring the big dark eyes.

Sally flung herself on the bed. "Oh, why did I try to say anything," she wept, "when I just got it all wrong? I only wanted to be a good friend, but she'll never believe it, never, never, never! Oh, I wish I hadn't said anything at all!"

The next morning, as they waited on the porch for the salesman who was driving them to Kirkland, Sally felt very hollow and lonely.

Mr. Barrett had already left for the shop, after shaking hands with Denny and giving Sally a hug and wishing them both the best of luck. Sally had washed the breakfast dishes and left the kitchen shining, with little "welcome home" and "we missed you" notes tucked around for Mom to find in the empty cake pan and cookie jar and on the almost bare refrigerator shelves.

Now there was nothing to do but wait. Dennis prowled nervously around the porch and front yard and garage, but Sally sat very still on the top step of the porch, almost wishing she'd never heard the word tennis.

What a summer it had been — and how hard she'd worked and practiced for just this moment! Sally hadn't wanted anything so much in her life as she'd wanted this chance to play in a state tournament. Now here it was — one more step on the road to being a champion, Mr. Cochran would say — and all she felt was scared and small and lonesome. And friendless. Wishing she didn't have to go.

"Here he comes!" Dennis called out.

A sleek car had rounded the corner and was coming slowly down the street as its driver looked at house numbers.

"Hey, how do you like that? Guess we're really going in style!" Dennis ran out to the curb and waved his racket wildly to catch the driver's eye. "Hurry up!" he yelled happily back at Sally.

Sally picked up her racket and suitcase and started obediently down the walk. The man at the wheel got out to take them from her.

"Looks like I've got the right place," he said, smiling. "I'll just put these things in the trunk and we'll be on our way."

Sally turned for a last forlorn look at the house as she got into the car — and saw a chubby, dark-haired figure racing down the block.

"Sally! Sally, wait a minute!"

Sally cried unbelievingly, "Floppy!" And then Floppy's arms closed around her in a strangling hug.

"I couldn't let you go without saying good-bye and good luck," Floppy whispered, "when it's practically the biggest thing that's ever happened to you."

"Oh, Floppy! Thank you — thank you!"

The salesman closed the trunk and went around to get into the car. Dennis waited at the opposite door impatiently. But Sally and Floppy just held each other close.

"Hey, come on!" Dennis urged. "For Pete's sake, we haven't got all day!"

"Yes, if we're going to make Kirkland by noon, we'd better get started," the salesman advised.

Floppy said hurriedly, "Here — it's for good luck," and thrust something into Sally's hand. Dennis pushed his sister into the car.

Sally hung back to say, "Floppy, I'm terribly sorry about last night. I was all out of line. I shouldn't have said —— "

"Yes, you should have. It's all right. I thought it over, and — it's all right, honest it is, Sally. That's the way it ought to be with friends. Good-bye, Sally, good luck!"

"Good-bye," Sally called back, blinking

tears out of her eyes to see more clearly as the car moved away. "Good-bye, Flop!"

Dennis said, "Anybody would think you were going to the South Pole — good grief! Look at you — you're just about bawling." He shook his head. "Girls," he said, not for the first time.

Sally looked down at the good-luck token Flop had thrust into her hand — Flop's most precious possession, the key chain that had been Jeff Donnelly's. To Sally it didn't look like a silly bit of metal anymore; Flop's love made it shine brighter than diamonds.

"What's that?" Dennis asked.

"My good luck," said Sally softly. "I'm going to pin it in my pocket so it won't fall out. And I'll wear it every minute of the tournament."

"That's a laugh," said Dennis. "Your good luck better be in your right arm, not your pocket. That's all I can say."

But Sally, with her heart light again and the familiar excitement at last stirring in the very bottom of her stomach, thought it wouldn't hurt a bit to carry her luck in her right arm *and* her pocket.

As the long miles streamed out swiftly behind them, Sally's excitement grew.

"Will they have made the draw already?"

she wondered aloud. "Oh, of course they will. Even at Maryville they had it all set up the night before."

She fell silent, thinking of her name on that faraway white sheet, matched up with some stranger's. Now nervousness grew side by side with her excitement.

"Are the courts like those at Maryville?" she asked Dennis. "Did Mr. Cochran ever say? It makes a difference in the way the balls bounce, whether they're gravel or black-top or grass. Or concrete. Oh, I hope they aren't concrete. Balls bounce too high on concrete."

"Will you quit chattering, for Pete's sake?" Dennis begged.

Sally looked sideways at him. His jaw was set tight, and he gripped his precious new racket so hard that his knuckles were white.

"Why, he's just as scared as I am," Sally thought in surprise, and felt her nervousness mounting inside her like a giant balloon.

They reached Kirkland at noon. Their salesman friend drove them straight to the country club where the state championship would be decided.

"When you want to get back downtown," he advised, "look for a city bus with 'Oak and May' on it. That'll take you right down past the YWCA and the YMCA. Good luck, kids."

They thanked him and stood staring wordlessly at the courts, which were already filled with players and all the action and excitement of a big tournament.

"Ohhhh," Sally breathed at last. "Oh, Denny!"

There were eight courts — a huge double row of gleaming, pale golden rectangles, smooth and clean as a waxed floor. Beside each court a referee perched on his lofty platform, and well behind the baselines ball boys and ball girls waited alertly to snatch up and return balls that went wild so the players needn't waste time and energy retrieving them.

"Denny," Sally said faintly, "I guess I never saw a real tournament before. I guess I never saw a real tennis court either. Denny, what if I don't even know how to play tennis?"

24 —————

"QUIET, YOU!" Denny growled at her nervously. "Whaddya want to let a tennis court scare you for? The better the court, the better you'll play."

Sally was unconvinced, but she shut up.

"Come on," Dennis ordered. "We have to report we're here and ready to play."

Sally followed him slowly toward the porch of the clubhouse, where an entry desk had been set up. She looked anxiously at every girl she passed, and felt more and more uncomfortable. Not another girl was dressed in tennis clothes.

The draws were posted on the porch near the entry desk. Sally looked for the one headed "Junior Girls." There was her name, linked with a girl from a town in the south of the state, "Ramona Brown."

Sally glanced at the top of the draw. Who

had been seeded number one? A Kirkland girl, she saw — Marjory Hicks. Sally had heard of her; she had won a lot of titles.

"And I'm in her half of the draw, too," Sally murmured. "If I just happened to beat this Ramona person — and won my second-round match, too — I'd play Marjory Hicks in the semi-finals. Think of it — a real champion!"

A shiver went down Sally's back at the prospect.

She joined Dennis at the entry desk. Their entry fees had been mailed in earlier; now, when they reported their names, the tournament manager checked them off his list. Noticing Sally's tennis outfit, he said, "Sorry we haven't a court open where you can practice. But I'm afraid they'll be filled all day with matches."

"Won't I be playing a match, too?" Sally asked.

"Not today. There are always so many more boys' matches to be played than girls' that we give them the entire first day."

"Oh," said Sally, understanding at last why she was the only girl there in a tennis dress.

She went over to the porch steps and sat down in the most out-of-the-way corner.

Here she was, all keyed up for action — her nerve bolstered to the point where she could *almost* tackle Marjory Hicks herself — and now all she could do was sit.

Dennis went past her, tight-lipped, gripping his racket hard, walking beside a boy his own size. Sally looked after him with envy. *He* didn't have to sit around, getting more scared and more tense every minute; he could *do* something. Win or lose, he could at least play.

An hour later Denny was back.

"I won!" he whispered excitedly to Sally as he passed. Lucky, lucky Dennis, Sally thought fervently, with that awful first match over already! To think he'd reached the second round of a state tournament! Mr. Cochran would be so proud.

Sally sighed and squirmed on the porch steps, trying to find a softer spot for her aching bones.

Dennis played and won another match before the afternoon was over. After that, he was like a balloon let loose; even Sally's increasing gloom couldn't hold him down.

"Boy, was my volley ever working! Hot as a firecracker! Wish Mr. Cochran could've seen it!" Dennis had never talked so much as he did that night over the tremendous dinners they ordered at a downtown restaurant. He described his victories point by point. "I got him in the corner with a drive, like this, see?" Denny's fork sketched out the shot on the napkin. "And then I came up fast and did a little cross-court volley over to here. I had him cold!"

Slowly Sally took fire from his enthusiasm. After all, her day of sitting was over now, wasn't it? Tomorrow she'd be out on the court, too, and it would be her turn — win or lose — to have a completed match to talk about.

"Let's get up real early, Denny," she begged. "Let's be out at the club by — by seven o'clock, and practice and practice and practice!"

"Sure, why not?" Dennis agreed. "Boy, we'll be so good, we'll mow 'em down!"

Sally was so excited at the idea of mowing down a state tournament that she hardly noticed her bill for dinner. Four dollars. That left Sally's total remaining fund for the tournament, now that entry fees and return bus fare had been taken care of, a good deal lower than it was before.

"Oh, well, that's okay," she thought a little nervously, counting her money later that night at the YWCA. "I probably won't be here longer than tomorrow. Anyway, I ate so much dinner tonight, I don't see how I could be hungry again for days and days."

Her dress was pretty rumpled from her day of sitting, Sally noticed as she put it on again the next morning, and had acquired a black smudge across the back, probably from the porch railing at the club. It was just a shame that she hadn't earned quite enough to buy a second tennis dress.

But maybe nobody would notice. It wasn't as if she was an important player who'd attract an audience.

Denny called for her before seven o'clock. They had breakfast together at the same restaurant (Sally was careful to order only orange juice and cereal) and then went straight to the club (bus fare, ten cents — another of the extras they hadn't thought to allow for, Sally realized).

"Oh, Dennis!" Sally cried when she saw the courts. The nets were down, and all eight courts were soaking wet. A crew of workers was still sprinkling the farthest ones.

Dennis said sheepishly, "I should have known they'd be fixing the courts for the day. In a big tournament like this, they do them all over fresh every single morning. Well, I guess we'll just have to wait."

To Sally it seemed that those were the only words she heard that long, long day. "You'll just have to wait."

The workmen told her that when she went out time after time to see if the courts were ready. The tournament manager told her that when she asked about her match.

"I'm sorry, Sally, but Ramona Brown hasn't showed up yet. You'll just have to wait."

Sally waited. After one brief, hard practice with Dennis in the morning before the courts filled with official matches, she sat around on benches and porch steps and the bumpers of cars — and waited.

In the afternoon Dennis played one match. Winning it put him in the Junior Boys' semifinals.

"What do you know, Sally, the semifinals!" he breathed. "Even if I get beat now, I'll know I'm one of the four top Juniors in the state! Isn't that something? Won't Mr. Cochran be tickled pink?"

"Mr. Cochran will be tickled pink about me, too," Sally thought despairingly. "I'm probably the champion sitter of the whole tournament!"

She put her hand to her pocket and felt the hard shape of the key ring.

"Come on, luck!" she said. But remembering how it came to be there — Flop's dearest treasure — Sally relaxed a little. She was lucky already, plenty lucky. Because she still had her friend, hadn't she? Even after she had gone off half-cocked, saying things that were far too big to be put into words, Flop was still her friend. A small miracle had happened, and Flop had understood what she was trying to say after all. That was good luck enough for anybody, whatever happened in the tournament.

That evening the tournament manager defaulted Ramona Brown.

25 ⸺

"CAN'T WAIT ANY longer for her to report in," the tournament manager told Sally. "We'll move you out to the second round."

There wasn't any chance of Sally's second-round opponent not turning up. She was already there — a big husky girl of fifteen with an unexpected booming laugh and all the confidence in the world. Sally looked at her when they were introduced, and shuddered.

They made a date to play their match early the next afternoon. Sally was out at the club from noon on, practicing grimly with Dennis on any available court, moving from one to another as a match was called on the court where they were playing.

"How's your racket holding out?" Denny asked her.

Sally looked at it. The strings Denny had

tied were still firm, but some cross strings were fraying badly.

"If *I* can hold out, it can," Sally told him.

Sally had skipped lunch. "I've got butterflies in my stomach," she'd complained to Dennis. "I *can't* eat." But that wasn't the entire reason. Sally's money was down to rock bottom. With her room at the Y paid up to tonight, she had only forty-five cents left besides the six dollars she'd carefully tucked into her suitcase for bus fare back to Fairfield.

"I won't worry about it," Sally decided, too nervous about the coming match to give thought to money problems. "If that huge thing with the loud laugh beats me, I'll be going home tonight anyway."

Home sounded pretty wonderful at the moment. Mom was home again now, and the house was probably filled with lovely tantalizing smells — cookies baking, and a pie cooling on the kitchen cabinet. Maybe a big thick chocolate cake in the pantry, with frosting half an inch high. Rich gooey chocolate frosting. Sally's favorite.

Sally's mind was on that chocolate cake when she served her first ball to Bounce Hilliard. She was thinking about it so hard that she served an ace. The big girl lunged for the ball without even touching it. She looked at Sally with new respect.

"Hey, what are you — a champ?" She laughed her huge laugh.

Sally's mind came back from the chocolate cake. She considered the big girl's question and sighed a little.

"Not yet," she admitted regretfully.

Bounce Hilliard had the sort of game Sally usually liked best to play against, a game like a boy's. She had a nice hard drive — no chops to worry about here — but Sally's was harder, and she could keep Bounce on the defensive, racing from one side to the other after the ball.

The first set was close; Sally took it, 7–5, and hung on to get a two-game lead in the second set.

It was mid-afternoon by that time. The August sun beat down hot and bright. Sally's stomach felt very hollow; the pale gold courts danced before her eyes.

Now and then she glanced across the courts at Denny, who was playing his semi-final match. Denny was scowling with concentration over each shot, and he looked as hot and tired and desperate as Sally had ever seen him.

The boy he was playing was tremendously

good, Sally decided, watching for a minute as she and Bounce changed sides. His shots fairly whistled, yet he didn't seem to make any effort at all.

"That's the way a champion looks," Sally thought, disheartened by the realization that Denny was losing. "Not like you, Sally Barrett — stumbling around the court with your tongue hanging out. Who ever thought you could be a champion?"

It was the kind of dream that was possible in a girl's own small home town where there wasn't much competition, and what there was, Sally could match herself against with confidence.

It was the kind of dream that went with a high heart and surging energy . . . a dream to be dreamed in a happy, comfortable home, with a loving family and friends saying that of course it was possible.

But out here on these strange courts filled with people all following their own dreams and not the least interested in hers — out here where the netposts danced before her dizzy eyes, and her dress clung to her with perspiration, and there was nothing, absolutely nothing, separating her backbone from her ribs but hollow, hungry space — how could she think about anything but getting out of here and going home where she belonged?

Bounce was tightening up, playing harder. Sally got no more aces or placements. She ran for every point, ran and hit the ball with all her strength, and ran still more.

Serve, drive, run to the net, volley, back up and try to meet Bounce's lob with a smash, watch Bounce incredibly get her racket on a ball that should have been out of her reach and loft it back again. Meet it and smash it again till at last it was put away.

Three-two. Four-three. Five-three. Slowly and ever more slowly, but steadily, Sally increased her lead.

Her head throbbed from the heat and from hunger. Her small stock of energy dwindled, and still she hung on.

Fifteen all. Thirty all. Sally glanced over at Denny's court and saw him shaking hands with his opponent. The boy started jauntily off toward the clubhouse to report the match — that meant he was winner. Denny walked slowly toward the bench, his shoulders slumped with tiredness.

Sally's heart hurt for him. She slashed into a service as fiercely as if she could beat Denny's victor as well as Bounce. The service went out. Sally started another swing, and then she saw it — the two frayed ends of her broken cross strings.

For a moment Sally stopped in mid-swing, staring upward in fury and dismay at those broken ends. It wasn't fair. It just wasn't fair! Wasn't it enough that she was hungry and hot and exhausted, and worried half to death about her money being almost gone, without this happening, too?

"Grief!" Sally muttered passionately. "Grief, grief, *grief!*"

With an angry swish she served her second ball and, heedless of the rapidly loosening strings, slammed shot after shot over the net to take the two final points with a barrage that left Bounce flailing empty air.

But Sally was close to tears when she went up to shake hands with Bounce. She had won, but what good did it do her — with her racket broken, her money gone, her one tennis dress a wrinkled, smudged wreck? What difference did it make when tomorrow she'd have to meet a champion who could probably give her five games a set and *still* beat her? It wasn't worth it, that's all. It just wasn't worth it.

Dennis walked over from the bench where he'd been putting his racket back into its press. He said, "Boy, that guy I played was

really something. You should have seen him."
He added tiredly, "I lost."

"Oh, Dennis!" Sally burst into tired, nervous tears. "I don't want to stay here any longer! I don't want to play tomorrow! Let's go home, Denny!"

Dennis gave her a startled look. "You mean you want to quit?"

Sally cried stormily, "I mean I *am* going to quit!"

26 ⸻

"AND DEFAULT OUT of the *semi-finals*? Are you crazy?" Dennis scowled. "You can't do that. Especially right after beating a kid out of *her* chance to play."

"I can, too," Sally wept. "Everything's gone wrong, and you know I'll get beat tomorrow anyway. So why do I have to stay? I want to go home!"

Dennis looked at her sternly. "Quit blubbering," he ordered. "Champions don't cry."

"I'm not a champion," Sally sobbed. "You said so yourself." But she took a quick swipe at her eyes with her shirt sleeve. "And anyway I want to go home!"

"All right," Dennis said unexpectedly, "go home, then — if you want to be a quitter. The bus leaves at six o'clock."

He swung off across the courts and Sally dropped limply onto a bench. Six o'clock.

Well, that gave her just time enough to get back to the Y and shower and pack.

Reluctantly she got to her tired feet again. Dennis hadn't waited for her. She knew she wouldn't see him again till she got on the bus; he was too angry to help her get ready to leave. Sally had depended on him these three days to steer her around. She wasn't even quite sure how to get back to the Y, but by luck she singled out the right city bus and reached familiar downtown streets.

Bathed and packed, her room key turned in at the desk, Sally stood on the street corner and counted again the remaining coins in her purse. Forty-five cents.

"I couldn't have stayed another day if I'd wanted to," thought Sally defiantly.

She felt light-headed from her long day on the courts and too little food. "There's time to eat," she decided. She'd have a hamburger. And a glass of milk. That would leave her a dime.

For what? "Fare to the bus station," she explained to herself.

But the bus station was only two blocks from the Y. She could walk there. Why not have a second glass of milk, then? She certainly had room for it.

But when the man at the counter set her

order before her and asked, "Anything else?" Sally said, "No." She clutched her dime tight while she slowly ate.

Champions don't cry. That's what Denny had said; the words kept going round and round in Sally's aching head. Champions don't quit, either. They keep plugging away, and getting beat by better players — until all of a sudden *they're* the better players. Champions.

"Remember, Sally," she could hear Mr. Cochran's warning, "it takes more than good shots to make a champion."

And now at last Sally thought she understood what Mr. Cochran meant. It did take more than good shots — it took courage, too. A stout heart.

"I'm not like that," Sally decided sadly. "I'm a — quitter."

She had come to the last crumb of her hamburger, and the clock hands had come almost to six. Sally picked up her suitcase and walked slowly out to the street. The bus station was to her left. Irresolutely Sally turned that way.

An "Oak and May" city bus was coming up the street. Oak and May. She and Denny had taken an "Oak and May" bus to the club this morning.

Suddenly Sally charged through the home-going crowd to the bus stop on the corner and surrendered her last dime to the "Oak and May" driver.

There, it was done. When she came back from the club again, it would have to be on her two feet, and that would never be in time to catch the six-o'clock bus to Fairfield!

A few matches were still being played when Sally reached the club. She watched until twilight ended them. Caretakers came out then, took down the nets, and sprinkled the courts. Sally waited until they began to roll up their hoses.

It was almost completely dark now. The last golfers had come in from the rolling fairways, the last tennis player had showered and changed and drifted off.

Sally slipped into a little summerhouse overlooking the first tee. Its back was to the clubhouse. Through the lattice she watched the workmen leave, and a long, long while later she saw the flashlight of the grounds keeper as he circled the clubhouse a last time before locking up for the night.

When he had disappeared and the clubhouse was a dark silent mass against the paler darkness of the night, Sally crept out of the summerhouse and up the steps to the porch. There was a big swing at one end, she remembered. She groped her way to it and stretched out gratefully.

"It's awfully quiet," she thought nervously. But then the sounds of the night gradually made themselves heard. A frog croaking down at the swimming pool. A friendly cricket chirping in a corner of the porch. A sleepy bird resettling itself in its nearby nest. Far off, the sounds of the city — auto horns, a siren, dance music.

"I'll never be able to sleep," Sally said, huddling deep in the back of the swing. "It's too scary. . . ."

27 =====

WHEN SHE OPENED her eyes, it was daylight and the grounds keeper was gently shaking her shoulder.

"Here, here, aren't you out pretty early, miss?"

Sally blinked. The sun was up. She could hear the patter of water as the workmen sprinkled the courts again. Grief, she'd meant to be out of sight before anybody came! Maybe people weren't allowed to sleep at the club.

"I guess I *am* too early," Sally faltered. "I was so — so awfully early I just went to sleep."

The grounds keeper let it go at that. He grinned in a friendly fashion and said, "You must be wanting to play pretty bad, miss. Must be an important match."

"Oh, it is!" Sally cried. "It's a semi-final

match. I've got to play Marjory Hicks, and she's a champion, isn't she?"

"Well, there was a time when she wasn't," the grounds keeper reminded Sally encouragingly.

Sally walked out into the sunshine. The night air had been damp and chilly; she felt stiff and cramped in every muscle. When the clubhouse was opened, she found a room where she could change into tennis clothes. She had thrown her tennis dress any which way into the suitcase last night when she packed; now she almost cried at sight of them.

"I'll look like something out of a ragbag," she mourned.

To keep as many wrinkles out of sight as possible, she crunched herself down on the porch steps after she'd changed, occupying a minimum of space.

People began to gather. The nets were put up, and the courts promptly filled with players. The tournament manager arrived with the big draw sheets under his arm and tacked them up on the clubhouse porch. Referees climbed to their little thrones. The state tournament was officially beginning its fourth day.

It was late morning when Sally heard a

girl's voice asking, "Where's Sally Barrett? Anybody here know Sally Barrett? I'm playing her in the semis."

Sally stood up slowly and went to meet Marjory Hicks. "I'm Sally Barrett," she said.

Marjory was tall and dark and slim; she looked about sixteen. Her tennis dress was immaculate pique, without a wrinkle in it. She looked at Sally in her crushed, none-too-clean clothes, and not the faintest sign of amusement or surprise disturbed her friendly smile.

"Hello," she said. "I believe we've got a match to play. How soon will you be ready?"

"I'm ready now," said Sally.

"Fine. We can get this first court here."

The tournament manager sent out a referee. He mounted the platform and announced loudly, "On the first court — a semifinal match in the Junior Girls' Division. Marjory Hicks, state junior girls' champion, Missouri Valley junior champion, playing Sally Barrett of Fairfield."

Sally felt as small and insignificant as her name sounded. Quite an audience collected to see Marjorie play, and there was a spatter of applause as the girls walked out on the court.

"Nobody even knows me," Sally thought

forlornly, "and they wouldn't clap if they did." She wondered what Denny had thought last night when he got on the home-bound bus and found she hadn't come.

"At least he knows I'm not a quitter," Sally consoled herself, "but — oh, dear, I wish he was here!"

Marjory served first. She had a powerful straight serve like a boy's. Sally blocked it, but its force nearly wrenched her racket from her hand. Marjory had followed her service to the net. She angled Sally's return away with a neat volley. Sally ran for it. Her heart pounded and her knees shook, but she got the tip of her racket under the ball and boosted up a weak lob.

Marjory stepped back, calculated its fall nicely, and smashed it for a placement.

Sally wobbled back to the baseline to wait for Marjory's next serve. That burst of speed had cost her her wind for a moment. She took deep breaths of air and tried to steady her knees. They felt like water.

"I'm hungry," she realized suddenly. "No wonder I can't run without falling to pieces."

Marjory's first service went out; her second serve was a much gentler shot that Sally returned with a vicious cross-court drive. Sally had put all her strength into that drive, but it hardly went deeper than Marjory's service line.

"Grief!" Sally thought. "I can't be *that* hungry!"

She tried again a little later — and again. Hard as she strained to lengthen her drives, they kept coming down too soon. Instead of forcing Marjory back to the baseline, they were allowing her to stand forward in the court within dangerously short distance of the net, where her volleys cost Sally point after point.

The points added up to three games lost, and Sally was just changing courts with Marjory when a blessedly familiar voice barked, "Here, you dope! Take this."

Sally grabbed for her brother instead of the racket he thrust toward her.

"Denny! You didn't go home!"

"Well, for Pete's sake, why would I? With you playing in the semis today."

"But you thought I was quitting —— "

"Aw, I knew you'd be here," Denny said gruffly.

"Oh, Denny, I'm so *glad* to see you!"

Denny growled with embarrassment, "I'm sure not glad to see *you* — patballing those baby shots. Why didn't you tell me your racket busted again?"

Her racket! No wonder her shots had been falling short. Sally had forgotten the broken string. Overnight her racket had lost much of its tension; now it had no more bounce than a feather pillow.

Sally grabbed Denny's racket. "Thanks, Denny!"

Denny's racket was heavier than Sally's, and the handle was a half-inch bigger around. Sally gripped it hard; it certainly didn't feel right. If she wasn't awfully careful to hang on to it, those balls Marjory hit were going to twist it right out of her hand.

She served cautiously, and met Marjory's return with a blasting forehand. The ball went clear to the fence.

"Yipes!" Sally gasped. "This racket's a powerhouse!"

Denny had had his racket strung much tighter than anything Sally had played with before. Sally was accustomed to pouring all her strength into a shot, confident that it couldn't go beyond the baseline. But now, with Denny's racket, her lightest tap sent the ball boys backing way up against the fence to catch her balls.

"Steady, Sally," Dennis whispered when she changed courts again, five games down now. "Hold back on them, for Pete's sake!"

But Sally, fighting the racket and the heat, her light-headed tiredness and growing panic, was fast losing her small stock of patience. Steady, hah! That was easy enough for him to say!

Her resentment grew as more points went against her. And then Marjory got over a whizzer, and Sally, blocking it too hastily, felt the racket turn in her hand. She dropped it like a red-hot potato.

"Ow! Ow!" she cried, shaking her blistered palm to cool it. The racket had twisted a bit of skin right off the ball of her thumb.

"Game and first set to Miss Marjory Hicks," the referee intoned. "She leads 6–0."

Marjory ran up to Sally. "Can I get you some tape?" she asked. "Would you like time out? I'll ask the referee."

"No, don't bother," Sally said crossly, but Marjory had already gone.

Sally slumped down on the sidelines and rested her swimming head against her knees. She was licked. Her hand throbbed with pain; she was dizzy with hunger; the increasing heat of the sun closed in on her breathlessly.

Why had she stayed in Kirkland last night, when she could have gone home? Six-love. Why, she wasn't even giving Marjory a battle! She was just making a spectacle of herself — Sally Barrett, a little nobody from a country town upstate, trying to play a champion!

Champion. How Sally had dreamed of being a champion herself! But champions didn't get there by dreaming of it. They fought. They fought until there was no fight left in them — like Sally now. And then they fought all the harder.

Sally's head came up slowly. She looked at the racket that had brought her nothing so far but grief.

"It's a gorgeous racket," she admitted. "If I'd only had time to get used to it . . ."

Time! Why, that was it! If she just had time.

28 ————

"HERE'S THE TAPE," Marjory said, hurrying back. "Goodness, I'm sorry about your hand. What a nasty blister!"

"It doesn't matter," Sally said. Her voice came out different somehow, more grown-up sounding. "A little blister's nothing to cry about."

She taped the blister carefully. "Just one more minute, Marjory," she asked.

Resolutely she walked over to Dennis. "My suitcase is on the porch, back of the swing," she told him. "There's six dollars in it. Will you take part of it and buy me some sandwiches, Denny? And a pint of milk. And a real gooey candy bar, or loaf sugar if you can get it."

Denny said uncomfortably, "That's bus fare, isn't it? How you figure to get home? I'm down to bus fare myself."

"I'll figure how to get home later," Sally said firmly. "Right now, I need that food."

Sally went straight to her baseline. "Ready when you are," she called.

Marjory served. Sally hung on to her racket hard. It mustn't slip again. Under the tape she could feel the steady throb of the blister. That was all right, though; it reminded her to hold that racket tight, tight, *tight*.

She met Marjory's service with a defiant chop — a hard chop that spun like a bullet off Denny's high-tension strings. But its underspin made it a shorter shot than a drive. It stayed in court.

Marjory apparently didn't like chops a bit more than Sally; she had to loop her drive to get her return shot over the net. That made it a higher, softer ball, and Sally mercilessly cut it down with another chop.

Chop, return — chop, return. Sally tried a drive again. It went out. Chop, return — the points dragged endlessly to add up to a game. Marjory's game. But the winning of it had taken her almost as long as the whole first set.

The girls changed courts. Dennis was waiting at the netpost. Sally took a big bite of the beef sandwich he held out to her, and a wonderfully refreshing swallow of milk. She tucked two sugar cubes into her cheek and felt them melt down her throat into liquid energy. Some of the hollowness inside her disappeared. The ground was firm and hard again, no longer floating under her feet. Now she served with new zest.

Chop, return. Chop, return. The patient points accumulated. Sally's service gave her a slight advantage. She took the game — the first game she'd won.

One-up. Two-up. Three-up. With each girl winning her own service game, they crept through the set. Again Sally tried a topspin drive, and again. They went out. Back she went to her steady, patient chop.

Four-up, and Marjory's service.

Marjory took the first point. And the second. Sally knew a brief moment of panic. "If she gets the games to five-four, she'll be just awfully close to winning." Only one service break away.

Desperately Sally tried another drive. The ball whistled low and hard across the net — and nipped chalk off the baseline.

"Yahoooo!" Dennis yelled.

"Grief!" breathed Sally.

She had won more than a point. She had won the right to drive — and drive — and drive — straight through to victory. The racket was licked.

And so was Marjory. Sally knew it that very moment. So did Dennis. And even Marjory suspected it, though she fought for every point until Sally zoomed a final placement to her backhand corner and the referee shouted, "Third set and match to Miss Sally Barrett of Fairfield. She wins 0–6, 6–4, 7–5."

Marjory ran up to the net to take Sally's outstretched hand for the conventional handshake. But there was no empty formality in Marjory's congratulations. She reached across the net to envelop Sally in a friendly hug.

"Sally, you were great! I'm *proud* to lose to you. You've got all it takes to be a winner!"

"She has that," another voice said contentedly.

"Mr. Cochran!" Sally gasped. "How long have you been here?"

"Long enough to see some mighty pretty headwork — and heartwork, too. Yes, it was well worth the drive down. I suspected one of you kids must be putting on quite a show down here, or you'd have been home before this. So I decided to see what was going on."

Dennis said proudly, "She'll win tomorrow, Mr. Cochran. It'll be a breeze. I've seen the other finalist play, and she isn't anywhere near so good as Marjory. Sally'll take her easy. Hey, what do you know, Sally — tomorrow you'll be a champion!"

Mr. Cochran looked at Sally's blistered palm, patted it gently before he released it. His glance was amused and tender and something more as he glanced at her rumpled, dirty dress and watched her wolf down the remaining sandwich.

"No, Dennis," he said, and to Sally his quiet voice rang out like a band on parade, "*today* she is a champion!"